"Listen, Ran," Jamie said to her best friend. "You know how Marylou's wedding is tomorrow, and none of our ideas to get me there have worked, and I was going to give up? Well, I've decided to put on my magic sneakers and sneak in!"

"Invisibly? Oh, Jamie, I think that's a terrible idea! You're going to get caught, I just know it," Randy cried. "The sneakers don't always work. What if you suddenly reappear in the middle of the cake or something? Oh, please, Jamie, I — "

"Randy, I promise you nothing will go wrong," said Jamie firmly.

Randy sighed. "I can see nothing will change your mind. Well, good luck — and I hope I see you soon."

"Of course you will," Jamie scoffed. "I'm not going to the moon!"

"I know," said Randy. "This is a lot more dangerous than that!"

#2
Wacky Wedding
Elissa Snow

PRICE STERN SLOAN
Los Angeles

ISBN: 0-8431-2723-6

10 9 8 7 6 5 4 3 2 1

Chapter One

"But Mom, why does Marylou have to have my *whole* room while she's here?" Jamie Keenan protested. "Why can't we at least share it?"

"Because she's your cousin and she's getting married in a month, that's why. A wedding is a very special time in a girl's life, honey," Mrs. Keenan explained to her daughter. "Marylou has a lot on her mind right now."

"So why can't she have a lot on her mind with me in the room?"

"Marylou needs privacy at a time like this," said Mrs. Keenan. "Besides, she's not used to sharing a room. She didn't grow up in a big family like ours."

"*That's* pretty obvious," Jamie grumbled.

1

Jamie was nine. She had two older sisters, Betsy and Margaret, and a younger brother named Tim. Marylou Mitchell, her cousin, was the only child of Mrs. Keenan's only sister. And as far as Jamie was concerned, Marylou acted like an only child — spoiled.

"It won't be so bad sharing a room with Margaret for two weeks," Mrs. Keenan said firmly. "I'm counting on you to be mature about this, Jamie."

Jamie tried one more time. "But Mom, why do *I* have to be mature when Margaret and Betsy are both older than I am? Why can't one of *them* be mature?"

"Because your room is bigger and it's closer to the bathroom. Now I don't want to hear any more about this, Jamie," Mrs. Keenan finished.

Jamie moved in with her twelve-year-old sister Margaret, and Marylou moved into Jamie's room with her five suitcases, her blow dryer, her exercise mat and workout tapes, fifteen bottles of nail polish, a silver-framed picture of her fiancé Nick Seldon, and a stack of phone numbers three inches high.

The only reason Marylou was visiting the Keenans now was that Mrs. Keenan was an interior designer. She was going to be decorating both the church where the wedding was to be held and the ballroom where the reception would take place after the wedding. So Marylou had decided that a two-week visit would be the best way to go over the decorating plans with her aunt.

"You see, Aunt Sue, I want to make sure every detail is *perfect*," Marylou said on the day she arrived at the Keenans'. Her blue eyes were wide with earnestness. "It's so important to me that I have a beautiful, beautiful, beautiful wedding. Do you know what I mean?"

"Of course I do," Mrs. Keenan answered kindly. "I think every bride feels that way—"

"No, not the way I feel it," Marylou cut in, shaking her blonde curls. "Because most people don't care about things in the deep way that I do — they're not as sensitive to atmosphere as I am. And, of course, they don't know how to arrange things the way I do. When I say I want this wedding to be perfect, I really mean it."

"Well, I'll certainly do my very best to make it as perfect as I can," said Mrs. Keenan with a smile.

"Not as perfect as you can!" Marylou answered sharply. "*Totally* perfect! Please, Aunt Sue. It's very, very important to me."

As the Keenan family soon realized, everything was very, very important to Marylou. It was very, very important that she be the first to take a shower in the morning before the hot water ran out, because she might get a chill if she took a lukewarm shower. It was very, very important that she read the funny pages first, because she needed to start her day with a cheery outlook. It was very, very important that she have Mrs. Keenan's car every afternoon so that she could shop for her trousseau.

And it was very, very important that Jamie do a lot of very, very important tasks for Marylou because — even with all the time Marylou spent in the car — she simply didn't have enough hours in the day to get all her very, very important business taken care of.

"Jamie, would you mind just biking down to the drugstore and getting me some caramels? I think I might have strained my throat yesterday, and caramels are kind of soothing . . . Jamie, could you please address these shower invitations for me? I want to put my feet up and relax for a little while . . . Jamie, would you mind clearing out your bureau? I'd like to put some of my new clothes away. Just take *all* your stuff out, would you? It's very, very important for me to feel as if I have enough space around me always."

"You know, Ran, it's very, very important that Marylou drop dead as soon as possible," Jamie told her best friend Randy Dowell one afternoon as they were walking home from school. "Sloshing" home was more like it. It had been raining all day.

Randy didn't even act shocked, which was unusual for her. She was so nice and polite that she didn't like Jamie to say anything mean, even when it was just a joke. But she'd met Marylou. "I know it. She's just awful," she agreed wholeheartedly. "How many more days is she staying with you?"

"Only three, but the time is just crawling by. Margaret and Betsy are going crazy because Marylou hogs the bathroom so much. Tim hates her because she keeps telling him to be quiet. Even Dad is starting to get cranky."

"You poor things, all of you," said Randy. "Want to come over to my house this afternoon?"

"I'd love to," said Jamie gloomily, "but I can't. I have to go help Mom cook. We're having Marylou's fiancé for supper on her last night here, and Mom's in a total panic about it."

"Well, maybe you can put on your magic sneakers and disappear," said Randy.

If it weren't for those sneakers, Jamie thought as she reached her block, I probably would have run away from home by now.

5

A month ago, Jamie's Aunt Letitia had sent her a birthday present that had turned out to be a pair of pink high-tops with fluorescent green laces. Jamie would have loved the sneakers anyway — but they were more than great-looking. They were magic.

When Jamie put the sneakers on, she disappeared. Not always right away, and not always for the same amount of time. Sometimes she reappeared gradually, in bits and pieces. Sometimes she came back the minute she took the sneakers off. But one way or another, they always made her invisible. And being invisible could be a big help when Marylou was around.

Unfortunately, Jamie was all too visible when she walked through the front door that afternoon.

"Hi, Mom!" she said. " — Oh, hi, Marylou," she added tonelessly. "I thought you were going to be shopping this afternoon."

"Well, I *was* going to be, but Betsy claims she needs the car," said Marylou in a voice that sounded a little too bright.

"I let Betsy have the car for field-hockey practice, Jamie," said Mrs. Keenan quickly. Betsy was sixteen, and she'd just gotten her driver's license. "It seemed so wet and clammy out that I didn't like the thought of her walking home after practice."

"But all that exercise would have kept her warm!" Marylou protested. "And anyway, I was only shopping for *her*! You know, Aunt Sue, I really have to pick out the presents for the bridesmaids *sometime*." Betsy and Margaret were both going to be bridesmaids in the wedding.

"Well, maybe the weather's a blessing in disguise," said Mrs. Keenan. "It will give us a chance to go over the new plans for the church. What do you think of these white satin bows for the candleholders, Marylou?"

"Oh, they'll probably be okay," said Marylou grudgingly. "I wish they could be bigger, though."

Mrs. Keenan's mouth was tight as she jotted down some notes. "So you'd like them to be bigger?"

There was a sudden clanging sound, and Jamie's five-year-old brother Tim came marching down the hall. He was wearing cowboy boots and banging a metal pot with a wooden spoon.

"Oh, the Grand Old Duke of Pork, he had ten thousand men," he sang. "Hey, Jamie! Want to see me — "

" 'York,' not 'pork,' Tim. Anyway, could you *please* keep it down?" said Marylou angrily. "Your mother and I are trying to accomplish something in here! Can't you go outside

7

or something?"

"But it's raining!" Tim protested. "There's worms all over the sidewalk!"

Marylou shuddered. "And *please* don't talk like that in front of me!"

"Talk like what?" Tim asked in a bewildered voice. " 'Worms' isn't a swear word!"

Marylou jumped to her feet. "Aunt Sue! Can't you control that child? He's trying to make me sick!"

Mrs. Keenan rose, too. "Come on, Tim," she said quietly. "Let's go make some playdough."

"Hey, great!" said Tim. "Let's make some playdough *worms*!"

"Sounds like fun," said Mrs. Keenan. "Jamie, do you want a snack?"

"Sure, Mom." Jamie followed her mother and brother down the hall to the kitchen.

Tim began banging on his pot again. "Oh, the darn old Marylou," he sang cheerfully. "She had a darn old darn . . ."

And Mrs. Keenan didn't even try to stop him.

The snack Jamie chose was three cookies and a bunch of grapes. She was still eating them in Margaret's room when she heard Marylou come flouncing down the hall and fling herself on Jamie's bed.

Then Jamie heard Marylou pick up the phone and angrily punch the number she wanted.

"Hello, Robin?" Marylou said in a second. "Is this a good time to talk?"

Robin, Jamie knew, was one of Marylou's best friends. She was going to be the maid of honor at the wedding. Jamie knew this because Marylou called Robin about once an hour.

"Oh, you're working on something?" Marylou sounded disappointed. "Okay, then. I won't take long. I just have to let off some steam. Honestly, this family! I don't know what I'm — wait a minute . . . let me close the door."

Wait a minute, Jamie thought. Let *me* put on my high-tops.

Quickly she pulled her pink sneakers out of Margaret's closet and laced them up. This time she was lucky. She vanished the instant she'd tied the second lace.

Lots of experience had taught Jamie that her door never shut tight unless you really slammed it hard. Marylou hadn't done that and Jamie gave the door a gentle push. It swung open, and she walked silently into her room.

"Oh!" Marylou clicked her tongue with annoyance. "This place is so drafty you can't even keep the door shut!"

She got up and closed the door again, more firmly this time. "And they don't even *listen* to me," she was saying. "Aunt Sue won't even *consider* any of my ideas."

What are you talking about? Jamie thought. Poor Mom spends all day listening to you! Angrily Jamie flung a grape seed at her cousin. It landed in Marylou's hair.

"Ugh!" Marylou squealed, patting her head frantically. "What *is* this? Oh, it's a grape seed. I swear, you can't even sit in your room in this house without *garbage* falling on you!"

She stood up and walked to the window.

"No, I haven't decided yet," she said, apparently in answer to a question from Robin. "Betsy and Margaret are going to be bridesmaids. But I don't know about the flower girl yet. It's very, very important to pick the right person, you know."

Jamie sat bolt upright. *I'm* the right person! she thought. I'd make a great flower girl! Marylou's *got* to pick me!

Her mind was racing in a thousand different directions. She could see herself marching down the aisle in front of Marylou, scattering a fragrant cloud of rose petals. She could see the congregation beaming at her and her mother wiping away a tear of pride.

"Who's *that* little girl?" people would whisper. "Really, she's even prettier than the bride! And she looks so much more intelligent!"

It would be great.

If I have to put up with Marylou, being a flower girl would be a very nice reward, Jamie told herself. It would almost make up for how obnoxious she's been since she got here.

All Jamie had to do was make sure she got the job.

Chapter Two

The homeroom bell rang, and Jamie's fourth-grade class began to straggle into the classroom. A few steps into the room — and everyone stopped in amazement. The place looked totally different.

For one thing, a thin layer of sand had been sprinkled over the whole floor. For another thing, Jamie's teacher, Miss Duni, was lying on her desk with her eyes closed.

Miss Duni was as still as a statue. Her arms were crossed on her chest, and her face had been painted to look like the cover on a mummy case.

"Miss Duni, are you all right?" asked Leesa Robinson shrilly. She was always trying to prove how much she loved her teachers. But Miss Duni didn't answer.

12

Several kids in the class walked up to Miss Duni's desk and peered curiously at her, but she didn't move. Not until the whole class had sat down did she rise slowly to her feet.

"I am a mummy — the essence of preserved time," she said mysteriously, and pointed to the blackboard.

On the board was a chalk drawing of what seemed to be a wobbly-looking dog wearing a woman's wig.

"All right, people," said Miss Duni in a singsong, faraway voice. "Look at me, and look at the drawing I've made. What do they tell you?"

She trained a piercing gaze on her fourth-grade class. No one raised a hand.

"Randy?" Miss Duni prompted. "Any thoughts?"

Randy shot a nervous glance at Jamie. "Um . . . It's — it's a very nice drawing, Miss Duni," she said.

"Thank you, but that isn't quite what I was looking for," said Miss Duni. "Any other thoughts? Jamie, what can *you* tell us? What does this drawing say to you?"

"The dog is . . . cold?" said Jamie hesitantly.

Miss Duni looked puzzled. "What dog, dear?" she finally asked.

"The one on the board. The one in the wig,"

said Jamie.

Miss Duni turned to see what Jamie was looking at. When she realized it was her drawing, she blushed.

"I guess I'm not really an artist," she said in a crestfallen voice. "That's not a dog, Jamie. It's the Sphinx."

There was an embarrassed pause before Miss Duni slipped back into her faraway mood. "And what does the Sphinx tell you?" she chanted.

Again, not a hand went into the air.

"Think pyramids," said Miss Duni. "Think desert. Think mummies. Think hieroglyphics. Think . . . *ancient Egypt*!"

She threw her arms triumphantly into the air as if she were waiting for the class to burst into applause. Instead, everyone just stared at her.

"Ancient Egypt!" Miss Duni exclaimed again. "The most exciting period in human history! And it's coming here — to our fourth-grade class!" Behind her round glasses, her eyes were bright with excitement.

Oh, no, Jamie thought. She glanced nervously over at Randy.

Miss Duni was a very nice fourth-grade teacher, but she had one problem: She got way, way too interested in things. She'd already subjected the class to six weeks of Bug

14

Sessions, when — as Miss Duni had put it — they'd had to "throw themselves into the world of insects." Jamie had been forced to spend the entire six weeks studying fruit flies with her worst enemy, Bill Baird.

If Miss Duni had wanted them to throw themselves into the world of insects, what was she going to want them to do with Egypt? Throw themselves into a tomb?

Well, nothing can be as bad as bugs and Bill the Pill Baird, Jamie reminded herself. This time around, I'm sure I'll get to — Leesa Robinson's voice cut into Jamie's thoughts. "It all sounds fascinating, Miss Duni!" she said brightly. "Could you tell us a little more?"

"Yes, please do! I'm also fascinated," added Larry Berman. Like Leesa, he always tried to show how much he loved school. Jamie sometimes wondered if he and Leesa were having a secret goody-goody contest.

Miss Duni gave Leesa and Larry a fond smile. "Well, you all remember Bug Sessions, don't you?"

"Yes," the class chorused gloomily.

"Of course you do. And you're all familiar, I hope, with the idea of *living* a subject instead of just learning it from dusty old books. That's what we're going to be doing with ancient Egypt. We're going to *become* ancient Egyptians."

From his seat behind Jamie, Bill Baird poked her hard between the shoulders. "You'll like that, Keenan," he whispered. "You're all rotten and moldy already."

"We're going to recreate ancient Egypt right in this classroom!"

"You can be the mummy, Keenan," said Bill Baird.

If Miss Duni heard him, she didn't show it. "Now, there were all kinds of people in ancient Egypt," she said. "Pharaohs. Servants. Magicians. Scribes. Priests. Farmers. Enough for everyone in the class to have a different role to play."

She pulled a piece of thick, crackly-looking yellow paper off her desk. "This is papyrus, one of the earliest forms of paper," she announced proudly. "I made it myself. The Egyptians invented it, of course. They made it out of papyrus plants, but since papyrus doesn't grow in New York State, I just took a paper towel and got it wet and spread it out to dry.

"The Pharaoh was the ruler of Egypt. Ancient Egyptians believed he was descended from the sun god, and he had absolute power. *Our* Pharaoh will be" — Miss Duni squinted at her sheet of papyrus — "Bill Baird."

"All *right*!" Bill shouted. "I have absolute

16

power!" He jumped to his feet and pointed at Jamie. "Off with her head!" he bellowed.

"Oh, no, no, no," said Miss Duni. "You must use your powers *wisely*, Bill. Now, of course the Pharaoh had a queen. Your queen will be Starr Stuart."

Oh, no, Jamie groaned to herself.

Starr Stuart was the prettiest girl in the class, and she knew it. She reminded Jamie a lot of Marylou — blonde, blue-eyed, and spoiled. Making her the queen of Egypt was the last thing Starr needed. It was like giving another tail to a peacock.

"The Pharaoh and his wife needed many, many servants to keep their palace in order," Miss Duni went on. "But we'll only have a couple of servants in this class, because there are so many other roles we need to fill. Jamie Keenan, you will be one of the servants. The two others will be . . . "

Jamie didn't hear the rest.

A *servant*, she was thinking disgustedly. Not just any servant, either — Bill's and Starr's servant. This is even worse than Bug Sessions. It's even worse than having Marylou staying with us. She'll be going home in a few days — but we'll be stuck in ancient Egypt for weeks!

"Jamie, here is something you'll certainly need for your job," said Miss Duni from the

17

front of the room. Jamie turned to see her teacher holding out a huge fan. "It got tremendously hot in Egypt — it still does — and the Pharaoh and his wife might ask you to fan them with this. If I were you, I'd carry it with me at all times. It's not wise to be unprepared around a Pharaoh, you know!"

"It certainly isn't," said Bill with a sinister leer.

"It's all right for you, Randy," said Jamie after school. "Being a musician won't be bad. At least you like music." Randy was going to be a court harpist. "But I'm going to be spending the next six weeks brushing Starr Stuart's hair and cleaning Bill Baird's desk!"

"Well — " Randy said weakly. Jamie knew she was trying to come up with something positive to say. "Well, maybe it will be interesting. If you have to be Bill Baird's servant, at least you're doing it at a cool time in history."

"I guess so," Jamie said grudgingly. "And maybe we can have the Nile River flood and carry the Pharaoh away," she added more cheerfully.

"Sure!" said Randy. "Why not? If that kind of thing really happened in ancient Egypt, I'm sure Miss Duni would think it was just fine. As long as no one gets hurt, of course," she added. Randy absolutely hated it when anything bad happened to anyone. "Hey, do you want to go over to the library right now and start doing some research?"

"Maybe later," Jamie said. "I need to forget about ancient Egypt for a while and start my flower girl campaign." Quickly she filled Randy in on the phone conversation she'd overheard yesterday.

"Wow, a flower girl!" said Randy. "I'm sure she'll pick you, Jamie. She owes it to you."

"I think so, too," said Jamie. "But it won't hurt to drop a few hints. Marylou isn't exactly a genius, you know."

Marylou was talking on the phone in the kitchen when Jamie got home. It sounded like another conversation with her friend Robin. Jamie's mother and Tim were nowhere to be seen. Maybe they were at a neighbor's house.

" . . . With lace all around the bottom," Marylou was saying, "and a big sash in back. And a matching hair ribbon — the hair ribbon is a very, very important touch. I think it will be adorable."

Is she talking about my flower girl dress? Jamie wondered. I hope it's not too ruffly.

She glanced around the living room. If I can just get Marylou to watch me throwing flower petals, she thought, she'll know I'm perfect for this.

But there were no flowers in the room. All there was was a big potted fern on the windowsill.

Oh, well, Jamie thought, that will have to do.

She stripped a few leaves off the fern and shredded them into petal-size bits. Then she walked slowly and gracefully past the kitchen, tossing fern bits around her in a little shower. Her head was high, and there was a misty smile on her face.

" . . . And maybe just a simple pearl necklace — Just a sec, Robin," said Marylou. She leaned out into the hall. "Jamie, what are you doing?"

"Oh, I don't know," said Jamie in a sweet, gentle voice — the kind of voice that belonged to a flower girl. "Just dreaming, I guess."

I did that just right, Jamie thought. But maybe I'd better do it once more in the kitchen, just so it will really sink in.

She went back to the living room and yanked off a few more fern leaves. Then she turned on the misty smile again and began gliding toward the kitchen.

I bet Betsy and Margaret will be jealous of me, she thought as she carefully dropped some green shreds onto the dining room floor.

After all, there are lots of bridesmaids, but there's only one —

"Jamie Keenan! What on earth are you doing?"

Jamie whirled around. Her mother and Tim were just coming through the front door. Mrs. Keenan's eye fell on the fern in the windowsill. "Have you been pulling apart my cobweb fern?" she gasped. "Jamie, that was going to be my exhibit at the flower show! It took me months to get it into shape! What on earth has gotten into you?"

Now that Jamie noticed it, the fern did look — well, kind of bald. I must have taken off more leaves than I realized, she thought guiltily.

"Sorry, Mom," she said in a tiny voice.

Mrs. Keenan shook her head with an exasperated sigh. "Sometimes I don't know what goes on in your head, Jamie," she said. "Get a dustpan and clean up this mess. And then I need your help in the kitchen, young lady. We're having company tomorrow night, you know."

Just then Marylou's voice floated out from the kitchen. "But I've pretty much made up my mind who it's going to be," she said. "I just decided this minute."

She *must* be talking about her flower girl! Jamie thought exultantly. That means she *did* notice what I was doing! From servant to flower girl in two hours! Jamie raced for the broom closet. "I'll clean this up right away, Mom," she called cheerfully.

For once Jamie didn't mind having her mother angry at her. If she ever got a chance to explain, she was sure Mom would understand. After all, it wasn't every day that a girl got to be one of the most important people in a wedding!

Chapter Three

"He's here! He's here!" Marylou screamed as she flung herself out the front door and ran down the steps.

It was Marylou's last night with the Keenans, and her fiancé was coming to have dinner. All day long Mrs. Keenan had been working frantically in the kitchen, and she'd made the four kids work frantically, too. A huge standing rib roast was waiting in the oven. Fresh flowers were everywhere. The bald cobweb fern had been banished upstairs. Jamie had polished the silver until her fingernails were black with tarnish, and her two sisters had picked every leaf off the front lawn by hand. (There weren't enough fallen leaves to rake, but Mrs. Keenan had thought the yard looked too messy the way it was.)

Now the Keenan family peeked cautiously out the living room window. Marylou's arms were around the neck of the biggest, burliest guy Jamie had ever seen. He was at least six-and-a-half-feet tall, and his neck was the size of a normal person's waist.

"Is that Nick?" she asked. "What a moose!"

"A moose?" Tim squealed joyfully. "Let me see!"

"No, Timmy!" said his mother. "It's just Nick! That's the man Marylou's going to marry, honey."

"Oh." Tim sounded disappointed. "Who's that girl?"

Behind Nick, a skinny little girl about six years old was getting out of the car. She was wearing a white party dress, white party shoes with real heels, and lacy white tights, and she had a huge white bow in her hair.

"I — I don't know who that is," said Mrs. Keenan. "Maybe it's Pauline. She's Nick's little sister. I wonder if — "

"Don't you think we'd better get outside?" inquired Mr. Keenan. "It's going to look pretty strange if we just keep lurking around in here."

"Aunt Sue, this is darling, darling, darling Nick," said Marylou rapturously as the Keenans came down the walk. Her arms were

24

still around Nick's neck. "Isn't he adorable?"

Mrs. Keenan didn't answer that. "It's so nice to meet you at last, Nick," she said. "We've heard so much about you."

Nick smiled and stuck out his hand. "Me, too," was all he said.

Quickly Mrs. Keenan introduced him to the rest of the Keenans. "And who's this?" she asked, bending down to shake hands with the little girl in the white dress.

"This is Pauline," Nick answered. "My sister. She — uh — she wanted to come along, so I said okay."

"It's lovely to meet you, Pauline," said Mrs. Keenan.

Pauline stared at her. "Mommy says Marylou's having terrible trouble with your plans for the church decorations," she said.

Mrs. Keenan blanched for a second, but she recovered quickly. "Oh, I think we've ironed it all out now. I'd like you to meet Marylou's cousins — Betsy, Margaret, Jamie, and Tim."

Pauline gazed critically at all four of the Keenan kids. "How old is Jamie?" she asked.

"I'm nine," said Jamie politely.

"Well, I'm six, and I *already* have pierced ears," announced Pauline. "Why don't you?"

"I — I just don't want them," Jamie replied. She'd always hated the thought of having holes put in her ears, but it didn't seem polite to mention that to Pauline.

"You mean you're not allowed to have them," Pauline answered knowingly.

"No, I could have them if I wanted. I just—"

But Pauline had already turned her attention to Margaret and Betsy. "Are you the ones who are going to be bridesmaids?" she asked.

"Yes, we are, honey," Betsy answered.

"Mommy says she just hopes you know how to behave yourselves in public," Pauline said. "She says nothing can spoil a wedding faster than a giggling bridesmaid."

The smiles on the faces of Jamie's sisters were a little strained. "We'll do our best," Margaret answered at last.

"Well, why are we standing out here when we could be comfortable inside?" Jamie's father suddenly said in a jovial voice. "Come on in, everyone!"

"What are we having for dinner?" Pauline asked the minute everyone was sitting down in the living room.

"Roast beef," said Mrs. Keenan. "Do you like roast beef, dear?"

"No, I hate it," said Pauline bluntly. "I hate all parts of cows."

"Oh, dear, that's too bad," said Mrs. Keenan. "Perhaps I could make you an omelette

26

or something — "

"I hate all parts of chickens," Pauline interrupted. "I'll just have some gum and some cocoa and a piece of bread with maple syrup. I'm very delicate."

"I — I see," said Jamie's mother. "Well, we'll do the best we can to find something you like." She turned to Nick, who hadn't said a word since he'd sat down next to Marylou on the sofa. "Tell me about your job, Nick. What exactly is it that you do for the phone company?"

"I work there," said Nick.

Marylou giggled. "Nick's not a big talker. He's more the strong, silent type." She leaned her head against Nick's shoulder. "My strong, silent hero," she crooned.

Next to Jamie, Margaret made a tiny gagging sound — so faint that only Jamie could hear it. Jamie barely managed to turn her laugh into a cough.

Mr. Keenan jumped to his feet. "That roast smells awfully good, Sue," he said. "I don't think I can wait a minute longer for it. Let's eat, gang!"

"So then I cried and cried until Mommy said I *could* have ballet lessons. And now my teacher says I'm the most talented student she's ever had. She says if there were a ballet

27

Olympics, I'd win fifty gold medals."

"Isn't that nice, Pauline," said Mrs. Keenan wearily.

"Yes. This cocoa isn't sweet enough. Could you put some more sugar in it?"

On the other side of the table, Marylou was talking as though she hadn't even heard Pauline. "So then I said, 'Well, I'll just try *one more* bridal shop,' and would you believe it? That's where we found the dress!"

Somehow, dinner with Marylou and Nick had turned into dinner with Marylou and Pauline. The two of them were perfectly matched. All they talked about was themselves — and meanwhile Nick said not a word. He just kept shovelling in the roast beef.

"It's lucky The Moose doesn't know how to talk," Jamie whispered to Margaret. "He'd never get a chance if he did."

Margaret suddenly snorted into her glass of milk. "Excuse me," she said when she saw Mrs. Keenan's eyes on her. "I swallowed wrong."

In a few minutes the conversation turned to Nick and Marylou's honeymoon.

"It's very, very important to me to pick the right spot," said Marylou. "So I think London would be best, or maybe Paris. You know, places where I can really soak up the atmosphere."

"You could try Alaska, too," Jamie murmured. "I hear there are *lots* of moose there."

This time both Betsy and Margaret snorted into their milk, and Mr. Keenan hid a smile behind his napkin. Mrs. Keenan glanced reprovingly at Jamie, but Jamie could tell she was trying not to smile, too.

"I hope you're not all coming down with colds," Marylou said peevishly. "I'd hate to catch one. But let's talk about something more important for a change — like the wedding." She reached for Nick's hand. "Now, I want to tell you all something very special. It's about my flower girl."

Jamie froze. Here it comes! she thought excitedly.

"As you know, it's very, very important to me to pick the right person for the job," Marylou continued. "And it's really because of my visit with all of you that I've been able to make up my mind. It has to be someone cute. It has to be someone graceful. It has to be someone I can trust not to mess things up. And that's why — "

Jamie sat up straighter in her chair.

" — And that's why I've chosen Pauline."

"*Pauline!*" Jamie gasped.

"Isn't it a great idea?" Marylou said. "I'm so glad she came along with Nick tonight. Now you'll all be able to look forward to how perfect she'll be."

"We — we certainly will," said Mrs. Keenan in an uncertain voice. She turned to Pauline. "Congratulations, dear. That's a big job!"

"Oh, I can handle it," said Pauline calmly.

"What's for dessert, Mom?" Tim suddenly asked.

Mrs. Keenan bit her lip. "Uh — chocolate mousse," she said.

Two minutes ago, that would have sounded like the funniest thing in the world to Jamie. Now all she wanted to do was get away from Nick the Moose and Marylou — and, above all, Pauline.

"May I please be excused?" she muttered. "I've got a lot of homework."

As Jamie walked upstairs to her room, she heard Tim ask, "Can I have Jamie's dessert, then?"

Jamie threw herself down on Margaret's spare bed. Her eyes fell on her magic sneakers, which were tucked partway under the bed.

Suddenly Jamie sat back up and reached for the sneakers. It might be fun to go back downstairs — invisibly.

After all, Jamie thought, if I can make Pauline look bad, maybe there's still a chance that Marylou will change her mind.

30

Quickly she laced up the sneakers and waited impatiently until she'd disappeared. Then she tiptoed down the stairs and into the dining room.

"Well, Pauline, there's not much mousse left," Mrs. Keenan was saying politely, "but if you really want a third helping, you may have it."

Quickly Jamie positioned herself by Pauline's chair. Just as Pauline was bringing a spoonful of mousse up to her mouth, Jamie grabbed the spoon and turned it upside down.

A blob of chocolate mousse slid down the front of Pauline's white dress like a garden slug.

"Gross!" Tim exclaimed.

Pauline stared down at her dress in dismay. "You gave me a broken spoon!" she said. "My mommy's going to be mad when I tell her!"

"The spoon looks fine to me, Pauline," said Jamie's father cheerily. "Maybe your hand is getting weak from all that sugar you've been eating."

"I *like* sugar," said Pauline. Calm once more, she picked up the spoon again and took another bite.

Behind her, Jamie was frantically swallowing air. Please, please let this work, she prayed silently. I know I can't always burp on command, but if it would happen just this once — Pauline finished her last mouthful and put her spoon down.

"*Uuuuuuuuuuuuuuuuuuuuuurrrrrrrp!*"

The sound was more like a foghorn than anything from a human throat. It worked, Jamie thought with satisfaction. Maybe the magic sneakers make me burp better, too!

Everyone was staring at Pauline now. Marylou was the first to speak. "Pauline, *please* try to control yourself!" she said. "It's really, really important that my flower girl not be a disgusting pig."

"I — I didn't burp," said Pauline. "It must have been one of the other kids. Probably that boy over there." She pointed at Tim.

"It wasn't me!" Tim said indignantly. "I heard that burp come right out of your head!"

"Let's just drop the subject, gang," put in Mr. Keenan. "I'm sure Pauline's sorry."

"But I didn't — " Pauline began.

Mr. Keenan ignored her. "If we're all done eating, why don't we go sit in the living room?" he asked.

"Yes, and I can dance for you while you all watch!" said Pauline.

Perfect! thought Jamie. She's really playing into my Invisible Avenger hands!

"You all sit down," said Pauline, "and I'll show you some of the things I learned in my last class."

Wordlessly the Keenans, Nick, and Marylou sat down. Not Jamie, though. She stood as close to Pauline as she could without touching her.

Pauline walked to the center of the room. "This my Dance of the Butterfly," she said, and she began to spin across the floor.

It took only a second for Jamie to reach down and grab her by the ankle.

"*Ooof!*" Pauline crashed to the floor with a tremendous thud.

"That was *lovely*, Pauline," said Betsy heartily. "What did you call it — Dance of the Sandbag? Thank you so much for showing us."

Slowly — blinking and breathing heavily — Pauline sat up and lurched to her feet. Then she glanced down. "My heel!" she wailed. "My heel snapped off my shoe!"

"Oh, dear, isn't that too bad," said Mrs. Keenan briskly. "That must have been why you fell. I guess that dancing in high heels isn't such a good idea for little girls, is it?"

"I'm *used* to high heels!" flashed Pauline. "Your — your floor is crooked! I hate this stupid house! I want to go home!"

Mrs. Keenan leaped to her feet. "You know, it is getting kind of late," she said. "It's probably a good idea for all of us to be thinking about bed." She crossed to the bottom of the stairs. "Jamie!" she called. "Come down and say goodbye to our guests!"

Jamie ran as silently as she could past her mother, up the stairs, and into Margaret's room. "Coming, Mom!" she called back. Then she wrenched off her pink sneakers and dashed back downstairs.

"Wow, Pauline!" she gasped in pretend amazement. "What happened to *you*?"

"Nothing," snapped Pauline. "Let's go, Nick." She tottered unevenly out the door toward the car.

"Bye!" Jamie called. "See you at the wedding!"

When *you're* sitting in the pews and *I'm* the flower girl, she said to herself. You don't have a chance now, Pauline.

Chapter Four

The invitation to Marylou's wedding was
lying on the piano when Jamie got home
from school the next day. It was engraved in
medieval script on thick cream-colored
paper.

A wedding is such a very special happening
. . . and that is why
Mr. and Mrs. James Lincoln Mitchell
hope you can share with them
the beautiful experience of
the wedding of
their daughter Marylou Dawn and
Nicholas Brad Seldon
on Saturday, October tenth
at half after one in the afternoon

"I bet you a million dollars Marylou wrote this," said Jamie sourly.

"She did," said Betsy, who was reading on the living room sofa. "I heard her talking to the printer on the phone. She said it was very, very important to make the invitation sound like a poem."

"Some poem," snorted Jamie. "Well, at least she's gone home. We won't have to see her again until the wedding."

Betsy put down her book. "Uh, Jamie . . . "

"What?" Jamie asked.

"Well, I guess you didn't see the reception card," said Betsy slowly. "Look in the envelope."

Jamie picked up the envelope the invitation had come in. Inside was a small card. Betsy was watching her nervously as she pulled it out.

Reception at half after two
Grand Ballroom, Rochester Arms Hotel

And in tiny letters at the bottom of the card were the words:

No children under ten years of age, please

"What?" Jamie shrieked. "I'm not even *invited*? MOM! WHERE ARE YOU?"

Mrs. Keenan came hurrying in, wiping her hands on her apron. "What's the matter, Jamie? Oh. I see you've read the invitation. I'm so sorry, dear."

"Mom, this can't be right!" Jamie said. "I'm Marylou's cousin! I've got to be there!" Then she suddenly remembered something. "Pauline is only *six*, and *she's* certainly going to be there! So there must be some mistake! Maybe the printer put in part of another invitation!"

Mrs. Keenan shook her head sadly. "I don't think so. Marylou's been talking all along about not having children at the wedding. She thinks it will spoil the fairy tale atmosphere, or something. I didn't mention it to you because I was hoping she'd change her mind."

"So you and Dad get to go — and Betsy and Margaret get to go—and stupid little Pauline gets to go — and I get to stay home with Tim and watch *game shows*?" Jamie was so angry her stomach hurt. "Mom, that can't possibly be right. I'm calling Marylou right now. Maybe she doesn't want other kids, but I *know* she wants me there."

Jamie stamped into the kitchen and punched in her cousin's number.

Marylou picked up the phone on the first ring. "Is that you, Nick?" she asked breathlessly. "The caterer called, and — "

"Marylou, it's me. Jamie." Jamie cleared her throat. "I was wondering if — "

"Jamie! Did the invitation come?"

"Yes, it did. That's kind of what I'm calling about — there's something wrong with the invitation. With ours, anyway. There's this line about no kids under ten years old being allowed. That's a mistake, isn't it?"

"No, that's right," said Marylou cheerfully.

"But you don't mean me, do you?"

"Well, you're not ten yet, are you?"

I can't believe this! Jamie fumed to herself. Aloud, she said, "What about Pauline? *She's* only six!"

"That's different," Marylou replied. "Listen, Jamie, this is all very interesting, but I'm waiting for a call from Nick, So if you don't mind — "

"Wait, Marylou!" Jamie's mind was racing. "I just remembered something. I really *am* ten! You know, back when I was four, I didn't talk very well, so my parents had me celebrate my fourth birthday twice! Well, that's a relief, isn't it? It would have been horrible if—"

"Jamie, no one celebrates a birthday twice except my mother," cut in Marylou. "I wish you could come, too. I know you would have loved to see me in my wedding dress. But it's just impossible. Now, it's very, very important that I touch base with Nick."

Click! went Marylou's receiver.

"And she didn't apologize?" Randy said wonderingly.

"Why should she?" Jamie snapped. "She wasn't even embarrassed! I can't stand this, Ran. After everything I did to help Marylou while she was here — and you wouldn't believe what a little brat Pauline is — and her stupid brother is a big dumb moose — and Marylou is being so disloyal — well, I'm not *going* to stand it. I'm going to get back at all of them!"

It was half an hour later. Jamie had stormed over to Randy's house right after Marylou had hung up on her. Now they were sitting in Randy's room angrily eating raw slice-and-bake cookie dough.

"Anyway, I've thought about it," said Jamie, squeezing another hunk of dough out of the tube, "and I've decided that the best thing to do is to put on the magic sneakers and set fire to Marylou's wedding dress."

"No, Jamie! You can't! That's too dangerous! Besides, I bet she'd just buy a new one," Randy objected. "I think the best thing to do is figure out a way to get invited to the wedding. Maybe you could ask Marylou's mother?"

"No. She'd tell Mom right away, and Mom would get angry at me for being rude. She says I just have to be mature and accept this."

"Well, what about . . . " Suddenly Randy's face brightened. "I know! Let's look up weddings in my parents' etiquette book. I bet there's some way you can wangle an invitation that *wouldn't* be rude."

She ran over to the bookshelf and took down a heavy volume with a photograph of a woman curtseying on the cover. "Here it is," she said, staggering a little as she carried the book over to Jamie.

"Wow, this has everything," said Jamie a few minutes later. "Listen: 'If you choke on a fishbone at a formal dinner, put a napkin to your lips and leave the room quietly.' What if you don't have enough time?"

"I guess it's politer to die, then," said Randy. "What does it say about weddings?"

The book said pretty much everything about weddings. But there was no mention of what a nine-year-old should do if her horrible cousin refused to allow her to come to the wedding at all.

"It's no use," said Jamie in despair. She slammed the heavy book shut and picked up the tube of cookie dough again. "There *is* no polite way to get Marylou to ask me. Okay, then — we need to think of a new strategy. What's a *rude* way to get her to ask me?"

"You know, Jamie," Randy said slowly, "from what you've told me about Marylou, she'll never ask you, no matter what you do. Why don't you work on your parents instead? I mean, if they told her they *had* to bring you, Marylou wouldn't be able to say no."

Jamie brightened. "That's a great idea, Ran! Let's see ... Pretend I'm my parents. You're me. What can you do to convince me that I've got to take you along?"

"Well, I could — I could say I was too nervous to be left alone," suggested Randy.

"But they'll probably say I can stay at your house while they're gone."

"Well, tell them you can't! Tell them you're too scared!"

"But I've spent the night here dozens of times! Why would they —" Then Jamie stopped. "Unless I start pretending to be shy right away," she said. "The wedding's not for a month. That should give me time. I'll just start acting more and more nervous about *everything*. They'll think I'm going through some kind of weird sensitive stage, and they won't *dare* leave me at home! Oh, Ran, that's a great idea!

41

"Pass me the cookie dough," Jamie went on. She was grinning. "I think I feel a little *nervous* without it."

Chapter Five

Mrs. Keenan peeked into Jamie's room the next afternoon. "Jamie, I'm running out to the store to get a quart of milk," she said. "Will you keep an eye on Tim while I'm gone?"

Jamie looked up from her desk and flinched. "Wh-when will you be back, Mom?" she quavered.

Mrs. Keenan looked perplexed. "In five minutes. Okay?"

Jamie's eyes were wide with terror. "No! Please, Mom, don't leave me alone! I can't stand it!"

The tears Jamie had cultivated by refusing to blink finally spilled over onto her cheeks. She stood up and hurled herself into her mother's arms. "Don't go, Mommy!" she wailed. "I'm too afraid when I can't see you!"

Mrs. Keenan patted Jamie on the head. "All right, honey," she said tenderly. "If you're really worried about something, I'll stay at home this once. We can drink juice tonight. Want to help me get supper ready?"

"Y-yes, Mom." Jamie wiped her eyes with a trembling hand and quietly followed her mother down the hall.

"It's working," she whispered triumphantly to Randy on the phone after supper. "Mom believed me!"

"Great!" exclaimed Randy. "What are you going to try next?"

"Well, I'm going to walk kind of hunched up, as though I were afraid to look people in the face. And I'm also going to wake up a few times in the night. When Tim does that, it always gets their attention."

"Oh, that sounds good," Randy agreed. "And you know what else you could do? Try acting scared at school. Maybe Miss Duni will tell your parents you seem insecure about something."

"Perfect!" said Jamie happily. "Will you help me?"

"Of course I will. I *always* like to help shy, disturbed people like you, Jamie," said Randy.

*   *   *

It was a peaceful, moonlit night, and the Keenan family was sleeping soundly when a piercing scream split the air.

"MOM! DAD! DON'T LEAVE ME! HELP ME! HELP ME! HELP — "

"I'm here, Jamie," said Mr. Keenan in a tired, croaky voice. He was standing in her doorway. "What's the matter, honey? Bad dream or something?"

"Oh, Daddy, thank you for coming!" Jamie whimpered brokenly. "Yes, it must have been a dream. An — an awful, awful dream. You and Mommy were going away and leaving me . . . going some place far away, or maybe it was just an hour away . . . and I knew I'd never see you again . . . " She gulped and burst into very realistic-sounding sobs.

"Jamie, it's the middle of the night. No one's going anywhere," said Mr. Keenan exhaustedly.

"But you won't ever, ever leave me alone, will you?" Jamie asked in a trembling voice.

"No, honey. At least — " Mr. Keenan broke off suddenly, and Jamie wondered if he was thinking about the wedding. "We won't leave you alone," he said firmly. "And that's a promise."

"Thank you, Daddy," Jamie whispered.

There's nothing like waking people up to

45

break their spirits, she thought as she snuggled happily back under the covers.

"Jamie, you're walking so strangely, dear," said Miss Duni the next morning. "Do you have a stomach ache?"

Jamie gave a frightened little gasp and hunched her shoulders even higher as she walked to her desk. "No, Miss Duni," she said without meeting her teacher's eyes.

"That's good. And your saying my name reminds me. Class, from now on I'd prefer that you call me Isis," said Miss Duni. "You see, Isis was an Egyptian goddess. She sat at the judgment seat with her brother Osiris to decide where people should go after they died. The way I see it, a teacher is the closest thing to a goddess most students will ever see. And, of course, it's up to me to decide where you'll all go after fourth grade, isn't it?" she went on. "Besides, I do sit at a desk all day, just the way Isis sat in the judgment seat. So all in all, I think Isis is a good name for me. And my desk can be *called* the judgment seat."

Jamie glanced over at Randy and raised her eyebrows, but Randy pretended not to see her.

"Now today we start an especially exciting part of our project," said Miss Duni. "We're

46

going to be building a real pyramid! I had a brainstorm at the grocery store the other day." She walked over to a corner of the room where there were some big flattened-out cardboard cartons. Then she picked one up and folded it back into a carton. Proudly she held it up to the class.

FLUFFIES TOILET TISSUE, said the label on the carton.

"Isn't that wonderful?" said Miss Duni proudly. "These toilet paper cartons are just the right size to be blocks for our pyramid! Now, I saw that a big shipment of Fluffies had just been delivered when I was at the store, so I know they have plenty. I want each of you to make sure to ask for empty cartons whenever you go to the grocery store, and bring them in to school with you. We need as many as we can get!"

An cloud of embarrassment so thick you could almost see it filled the air. Every member of the class was trying to imagine what it would be like to carry Fluffies cartons on the school bus.

"Okay," said Miss Duni. "Which of you did I assign to be outdoor servants to Pharaoh Baird?"

Leslie Turow, Peter Lawrence, and Todd Hauser stood up — very slowly.

"I'm putting you three in charge of building the class pyramid," said Miss Duni. "You can get started right away. And make sure it goes right up to the ceiling!"

"Uh, Miss Duni — I mean Miss Isis — how are we supposed to build it?" asked Peter. "Should we glue the cartons together, or what?"

"Just 'Isis' is fine, Peter," said Miss Duni. "Well, no one really knows how the ancient Egyptians built the pyramids. So whatever way you want to make yours is fine — as long as *we* don't know how you did it, either!"

The three outdoor servants stared at her helplessly. "All right, Miss Isis," said Leslie after a second.

"Just 'Isis' is fine," Miss Duni repeated. "No one calls a *goddess* 'miss'!"

"Servant! Come and fan me instantly!" shouted Pharaoh Baird.

With a sigh Jamie picked up her fan and moved slowly toward his desk.

It was a hour later, and ancient Egypt was going strong in Miss Duni's classroom. Leslie, Peter, and Todd were standing in the corner arguing about the best way to stack the Fluffies cartons. Mike Liu — who'd been assigned the role of scribe — was writing hieroglyphics on the blackboard. Randy was at the Pharaoh's feet dreamily humming to herself and strumming the harp Miss Duni had made by wrapping rubber bands around a coathanger.

As she walked toward Bill's desk, Jamie realized that Miss Duni was watching her. This would be a perfect time to act insecure!

She hunched up her shoulders and walked cringingly toward Bill. "You wanted me to fan you?" she asked in a timid voice.

"That's what I said, isn't it?" Bill said loftily.

Miss Duni was still staring at Jamie, and she looked perplexed. She's noticed that something's wrong with me, Jamie thought. Good!

"Servant, why are you acting so sneaky?" Bill suddenly growled.

Jamie gave a startled leap backward. "I — I'm sorry," she faltered. I should get an Oscar, she was thinking. "I didn't mean to — "

"You've been acting weird all day," Bill interrupted. "Have you stolen something from my royal treasury?"

Wait a minute! Jamie said to herself. I'm doing this act for Miss Duni, not Bill!

Quickly she straightened up and started fanning. "I haven't stolen anything, your Majesty," she said in a normal voice.

"*I* think you have," Bill answered menacingly. "You have a guilty look. And I don't

like your attitude today. I'm switching your job, servant. I want you to go and help the outdoor servants build my pyramid."

"You can't *do* that!" Jamie protested. "I'm a Palace servant! Miss Duni said so!"

Bill smiled blandly at her. "And I'm the Pharaoh. Miss Duni said so. And the Pharaoh can make any of his servants do anything he wants. *Miss Duni said so*. Now, get over to that pyramid. And be sure to bring some Fluffies cartons to school tomorrow. Lots of them."

"I can't take our Pharaoh much longer," Jamie told Randy angrily as they walked home from school. "I don't *care* if Miss Duni lets him get away with this stuff — I'm not going to. It's time to pay him back a little. Wasn't there some kind of curse on King Tut's tomb?"

"I think so," said Randy. "I read somewhere that the guys who discovered the tomb all died mysteriously."

"Let's find out more about it," said Jamie. "I know I'm only a humble servant, but I could do a lot with a curse like that."

"What do you mean?" asked Randy blankly. "Who do you want to put a curse on?"

"Why, our beloved Pharaoh, of course," said Jamie. "Who else?"

51

Randy looked worried. "But Jamie, we can't put a curse on Bill! He might get hurt, and we'd wind up in jail! My parents would be so mad at me!"

"Oh, Randy!" Jamie groaned. "Do you really think any curse we'll find in a history book will actually *work*? I just want to do something to get back at him."

"Oh," said Randy. "Well, I guess that's okay, then. As long as we don't get in trouble."

"I guarantee that we won't," Jamie answered. "Now, do you want to go to the library before we head home?"

As Jamie walked home from the library, she was feeling much happier. The books she and Randy had found hadn't exactly told them how to make a curse, but she was sure Miss Duni would let her do some more research.

"Hi, Mom," she said cheerfully as she walked through the front door.

"Don't take your coat off," her mother ordered. "We're going straight to the doctor's."

"Why? Are you sick?" asked Jamie.

"No. I want him to look at *you*. Jamie, Miss Duni called today. She's worried about you."

"She is?" asked Jamie. *All right!* she wanted to shout.

"Yes. She thinks you may have a posture problem. She says you were walking all hunched up in class, and she says we should ask a doctor if you need a brace for your back."

Oh, no, thought Jamie. So *that's* why she was staring at me. Not because she thought I was insecure at all!

"Actually, I'm glad she called when she did," said Mrs. Keenan, "because I've been worried about you too. It seems to me you haven't been acting like yourself these past few days. Are you worried about me and Daddy going to the wedding?"

This is the best chance I'll have, thought Jamie. I'm going to give it all I've got.

She opened her eyes wide, shrank nervously back from her mother, and bit her lip. I'm a frightened fawn, she told herself. A little fawn, trembling in the woods. . . .

"Yes," she said in a whisper. "That's what I'm worried about."

"That's what I thought," said her mother gently. "Well, honey, you don't have to worry any more. I was going to have you stay with Randy while we were gone, but since you're so upset I won't do that. I'll hire old Mrs. Proutie from down the street to be your babysitter instead."

Chapter Six

"Well, *that* idea sure backfired," said Randy glumly as she and Jamie walked to school the next morning. "I'm sorry I suggested that you act scared in front of Miss Duni."

"It wasn't your fault," said Jamie. "And at least the doctor didn't make me wear a back brace. He told Mom there was nothing the matter with me and that Miss Duni must be crazy. I could have told her *that* myself."

Randy sighed. "It would have been so much fun to have you stay at my house, though. Well, maybe it won't be so bad having Mrs. Proutie taking care of you — "

"Are you kidding?" Jamie interrupted. "No, there's no way I'm going to spend even an hour with Mrs. Proutie. I'm going to the wedding, Ran."

"You are? But Jamie, how? You aren't planning anything bad, are you?"

"No, no," said Jamie impatiently. "I've thought of a new plan, that's all. You know how I never spend my allowance? Well, I've got a *lot* of money saved up, and I'm going to spend it on a wedding dress. I mean, a dress I can wear to the wedding. I'm buying it on the weekend. Want to come along?"

"But I thought Marylou said — "

"I know what she said," Jamie interrupted again. "But look, Ran. If you were Marylou, and your dear, dear little cousin had gone out and spent three years' worth of allowance on a beautiful dress, wouldn't you let her into the wedding?"

"*I* would," said Randy after a pause. "But I don't know if Marylou would."

"Well, she will," said Jamie confidently. "When Marylou sees me in this dress, she'll realize her mistake right away."

"This is it," said Jamie on Saturday morning. "Jacqueline's Wedding Parlor." She and Randy parked their bikes outside the store and peered into the window.

"It looks pretty fancy," said Randy doubtfully.

It certainly did. The bride mannequin in the window was wearing a white mink wedding dress.

"Well, I've got plenty of money," said Jamie. "And I *want* something fancy. I've got to look better than Pauline, don't forget."

"But we're in jeans!" Randy wailed. "They'll think we're slobs! You go in and buy the dress, Jamie. I'll wait out here and — uh — and guard our bikes."

"Oh, Randy, stop worrying and come *on*," said Jamie. She grabbed Randy's wrist and pulled her through the door.

Inside, the store was hushed and dim, like a chapel. Jamie and Randy squinted through the darkness, trying to get their bearings.

"May I hailp you, geerls?" someone said instantly.

A smiling young woman with an accent Jamie couldn't quite identify was coming toward them. "Are you Jacqueline?" Jamie asked.

The woman's smile became even sweeter. "No, no. I am only Marie."

"Well, we'd like to look at your dresses for flower girls," said Jamie.

"Sairtenly. And for which wedding is this?"

"Well, it's my cousin's wedding. But I'm — I'm kind of a substitute flower girl, actually. I'm picking out the dress myself."

Marie's smile wavered, and she shrugged

ever so faintly. "The flower geerls' dresses are over here," she said, leading them to a rack on the opposite wall. "And I think you will find that they are vairy, vairy special."

"Oh, Jamie, these are beautiful!" Randy gasped when she saw the row of dresses. "You're so lucky!"

Jamie didn't feel lucky. Randy loved dresses, but Jamie hated them — and these were so fancy that they looked as if they were wearing dresses of their own.

The saleswoman reached forward and pulled what looked like a pile of hot-pink ruffles off the rack. "Pairfect for a young geerl! It has hoop skirts and a matching parasol! Vairy, vairy sharming."

The dress had more than that. It also had lace and seed pearls and satin bows and fake flowers and elbow-length hot-pink gloves. *And* it was strapless.

"I — I don't think — " Jamie began.

"And see, it comes with its own hat," said Marie coaxingly. "Don't you think those plumes are *elegant*? And the veil — so fetching!"

"It's beautiful," Randy breathed. Her face was glowing with admiration.

"Your friend has good taste, I see," said Marie. "Trust us, miss. You'll outshine everyone else at the wedding."

57

Including Pauline ...

"All right," said Jamie. "I'll take this one. How much does it cost?"

Marie leaned forward and murmured something into her ear.

Jamie gulped. Then she picked up her purse.

"I hope you have a lot of time," she said. "Because I'm going to be paying in quarters."

"Mom, are you busy?" Jamie peeked into the living room, where Mrs. Keenan was working on some sketches.

"Sort of, honey," her mother answered absently. "I'm trying to finish these designs for Marylou's and Nick's reception."

Jamie leaned over her mother's shoulder to see. "They look great," she said. "But don't you want to put in a cage for Moose?"

"J-Jamie!" Mrs. Keenan giggled, then tried to look stern. "That's no way to talk about your cousin's fiancé!"

"Sorry, Mom," Jamie said. "Anyway, this won't take long. Mom, I — I bought something today."

"Oh, you did? You mean you finally spent some of your allowance?"

"Well — not some of it. All of it." Jamie took a deep breath. "I bought a dress."

"A *dress*?" Now Jamie had her mother's

full attention. "That's certainly a first! What's the dress for?"

"Well — it's for Marylou's wedding."

"*What?*"

Somehow this was turning out to be harder than Jamie had expected. "Well, you know how disappointed I was not to be invited," she said haltingly. "And how mad I was that Marylou picked Pauline instead of me to be flower girl."

Her mother nodded.

"Well, I thought that — um — if I chose a fancy dress and bought it with my own money — and if it was really perfect for a wedding — then maybe you'd talk Marylou into letting me come," Jamie finished in a rush.

Mrs. Keenan was staring at her as if she'd lost her mind. "You bought a formal dress on your own?" she asked slowly. "Well, you'd better let me see it."

Jamie raced upstairs to her room, where the dress, hat, and parasol were waiting on her bed. She put on the dress and hat, unfurled the parasol, and ran back downstairs.

Mrs. Keenan stared at her daughter — and then burst into shrieks of laughter.

"*Mom!*" Jamie gasped.

"I — I'm sorry, honey," said her mother shakily. "It's just that — that's the tackiest thing I've ever seen. Look at the *hat*!" She went off into another fit of laughter. "And that *color*! Jamie, what made you think you could wear hot pink with your red hair?" Tears were streaming down her cheeks.

"The saleswoman said it was perfect on me!" Jamie wailed.

"I bet she did." Mrs. Keenan cleared her throat. "She'd probably been praying she'd find someone she could unload it on. Okay, okay, honey. I'm sorry if I hurt your feelings. But really, that's the *most* inappropriate dress for someone your age that I've ever seen. How much did it cost you, anyway?"

Jamie leaned forward and whispered the total into her mother's ear.

"Oh, no." All traces of laughter vanished from Mrs. Keenan's face instantly. "Oh, that's not funny at all. That's — that's practically criminal. That's deceiving a minor, in my opinion. You'll have to return it on Monday and get your money back. I'll come with you if you want."

"I can do it alone," Jamie said with dignity. "No need to trouble yourself, Mother."

Jamie straightened her hat and started to sweep grandly away. Unfortunately, she tripped on her parasol just before she was out of the room.

It didn't improve her mood any to hear her

mother start whooping again.

It was Monday afternoon. School had just let out, and Jamie was racing for the school bike racks. Instead of putting the hot-pink dress in her locker, she had left it in her bike basket by mistake. Ominous gray clouds were gathering in the sky, and Jamie wanted to make sure she got the dress back to the store before it started to rain.

As she rounded the corner, Jamie stopped dead. Bill Baird was standing next to her bike, surrounded by a group of his friends — all of whom were laughing hysterically. The silver bag from Jacqueline's Wedding Parlor was lying crumpled on the ground. And Bill Baird was wearing the hot-pink dress.

"Oh, no," Jamie moaned. "Give me that dress!"

"But it looks so nice on *me*! It makes me look like a strawberry shortcake!"

"Bill, that dress cost a lot of money," Jamie said through her teeth. "Give it back to me right now."

"Uh-uh-uh!" Bill shook the parasol at her. "Remember who you're talking to! The Pharaoh can do whatever he likes!"

"Besides, didn't Egyptian guys wear those kind of skirt things anyway?" asked one of his friends.

"Yeah, I think so," said Bill. "So if you don't mind, Keenan, I think I'll just borrow this for a little while. Miss Duni will probably give me extra credit when she sees it."

He waved the parasol again. "Ta-ta," he simpered, and began to walk mincingly away.

He'd gone only a few steps when he tripped over the parasol just the way Jamie had. The hot-pink hat went sailing through the air, and Bill crashed to the ground face first.

Jamie stared at him in horror. The pink dress had torn at the neckline, and it was completely covered with mud.

"I hope you're satisfied," Jamie spat out. "You're wearing the most expensive rag in the country. Take a look at the price tag on the sleeve, Pharaoh."

For a second Bill looked a little scared. Then his face cleared. "If you didn't want anything to happen to it, why did you leave it in your bike basket?" he asked.

"Well, why *did* you?" asked Mrs. Keenan an hour later as she surveyed the ruined dress.

"I just forgot," said Jamie miserably. "Is there any way you can fix it, Mom?"

"Well, I can clean it up and mend the tear, but you certainly can't return a dress to the store in this condition," said her mother. She shook her head regretfully. "We can't let something this expensive go to waste, either. I guess it will just have to be your party dress until you outgrow it."

Mrs. Keenan gathered up the pile of hot-pink ruffles and left Jamie alone in her room.

Okay, thought Jamie grimly. First chance I get, it's curse time for Pharaoh Baird. He's going to be sorry he ever met me.

But I'm not going to let a wrecked dress keep me from being at that wedding, she vowed to herself. I'm *still* going. There's got to be a way to get there — and I'll find it!

Chapter Seven

One of the nicest things about Randy was that when Jamie had bad luck, Randy usually felt even worse than Jamie did. She actually burst into tears when Jamie told her what had happened to the hot-pink dress.

"Th-that beautiful gown *ruined*?" she wept. "Oh, Jamie, and you looked so beautiful in it! Just like a fairy princess! Oh, I can't stand this! Wh-where's the frosting?"

They were eating canned fudge frosting for their afternoon snack.

"Here you go," said Jamie, passing her the can and the spoon. "But really, Ran, don't worry. I'm not feeling that bad now. I never liked the dress much anyway. Of course, Bill the Pill is going to have to suffer for this," she added sternly.

"Of *course* he is," Randy said through a mouthful of frosting. She sounded shocked at the very idea that he might not have to. "Let's figure out how to put a curse on him *today*. Will your parents let you study at the library after supper?"

"I'm sure they will," said Jamie. "I bet Betsy will take us. She's on another diet, and she keeps looking for excuses to leave the house so she won't get tempted to raid the refrigerator."

When Betsy dropped the girls off after dinner, Jamie and Randy headed straight for the reference section. There they hunted up a big stack of books about ancient Egypt and sat down to look through them at one of the tables.

"Well, *The Curse of King Tut* says that the guy who found the tomb had a canary that was eaten by a cobra right after the tomb had been discovered," said Jamie. A pleasurable shiver ran down her back. "Then his partner died right after that of a mysterious mosquito bite."

"A mosquito bite?" asked Randy. "How could that kill him?"

"They think it had some kind of disease or something. Anyway, then a plague broke out in Egypt, and four other people connected with finding the tomb also died. And an old

66

man jumped out the window and then — "

"Stop!" Randy said. "I believe you! I think this is too dangerous to be fooling around with, Jamie. We could be arrested for murder!"

"Oh, we're not going to *kill* Bill!" Jamie reassured her. "We're just going to — to curse him a little."

But how? The book didn't really explain how the curse — if there had really been a curse — had worked. Jamie sighed. "I wish they'd give us the instructions," she said. "It's really frustrating to — "

"Here's a curse!" said Randy suddenly. "I mean, the *words* of a curse, anyway. They were written on a mummy case in the tomb of Amenhotep, whoever *he* was. It's not King Tut, but maybe it will still come in handy. Listen: *May the cobra on my head spit flames of fire into thy face, and may thy head be in the place of my feet. Such a curse is the vengeance which is hidden in my body throughout all eternity, and which shall overtake whomsoever disturbs my body in its tomb. He or she shall have no grave, and after an arduous journey shall be attacked by wild beasts, and his or her bones shall be left to be washed by the falling rain.*"

Randy and Jamie stared at each other. "Sounds pretty curse-y, all right," said

Jamie. "I like the part about being attacked by wild beasts." She bent her head to reread the curse in Randy's book.

"Hey, look at this!" said Jamie suddenly. She was pointing to a picture of a woman with what looked like a big trapezoid-shaped hat on her head. "That's Isis. She's the one who Miss Duni's supposed to be."

Randy glanced over her friend's shoulder. "Uh-huh," she said without much interest.

"It says here that she was the goddess of fertility," Jamie continued.

"Gross!" Randy squealed.

"I know it's gross, but — well, wouldn't that have made her sort of important at Egyptian weddings?" asked Jamie.

"I guess so."

"Well — this probably sounds stupid, but, uh — but what if we — you know — sort of prayed to her or something? I mean, if we asked her to help me get to Marylou's wedding *and* asked her to curse Bill for us?"

"Pray to an *Egyptian goddess*? Jamie, that's the craziest thing I ever heard!"

"*Quiet* in the library, *please*," said Mrs. Finch.

Jamie was starting to get excited about the idea. "The worst that could happen would be that *nothing* would happen! See, we could take a picture of Isis and make a sort of altar in front of it and maybe kneel down and *beg* her to help us, and — and then see what would happen."

"But what about — you know — the other God?" Randy faltered. "It doesn't seem like good manners to go around praying to an old leftover Egyptian god when there's a perfectly good modern one we could use."

"Well, our God's known about this wedding for months and hasn't done a thing to get me invited," Jamie answered tartly. "Come on, Randy. It might be kind of fun. And we could use a picture of Miss Duni in our shrine. *That* would certainly be modern."

"Okay, girls," said Mrs. Finch. "That's enough talking. Out you go."

"You want to take my picture, Jamie?" asked Miss Duni. She had taken to wearing long, long necklaces of salt-dough beads she'd made herself and painted gold. She also wore an Isis hat made out of newspaper, sandals, and a flannel nightgown — "my royal robe," as she called it — to school every day now, and behind her glasses her eyes were heavily outlined with black.

"Well, how nice!" Miss Duni sounded genuinely flattered. "Where would you like me to stand?"

"How about in front of the pyramid?"

Jamie asked.

The Fluffies-carton pyramid was really coming along. Of course it didn't look much like a pyramid yet — just a flat stack of boxes. Leslie, Peter, and Todd had managed to get it about halfway to the ceiling, but they couldn't figure out how to get it pointed on the top.

Now Miss Duni walked in front of the cartons. "Do you want me to kneel?" she asked.

"No, I think standing would be more regal," Jamie said. "And could you try to be sort of solemn?"

Miss Duni folded her arms across her chest and stared sternly into the air. "You know, when I stand like this, I really feel as though her spirit has entered me," she remarked.

The camera clicked.

One shrine photo coming up, thought Jamie.

"What did you bring to put in front of the shrine?" Jamie asked Randy as she propped the photograph of Miss Duni against her bureau.

"Well, I wasn't sure what you meant by 'treasures,'" Randy answered. "So I just brought some of my favorite stuff." She reached into the shopping bag she'd brought with her and pulled out her diary, a silver

necklace, a china horse, and a turtleneck with tiny pink hearts on it. "Are these okay?"

Jamie eyed the collection doubtfully. She wasn't sure how Isis felt about turtlenecks. "Well, the stuff I got was more the kind of thing I thought an ancient Egyptian might use," she said. She gestured toward a pile of cinnamon sticks, a vial of perfume, a brass candlestick, and a length of red ribbon. "But I'm sure Isis knows it's the thought that counts. Thanks, Ran." She arranged Randy's stuff in front of the picture of Isis.

"I got some incense, too," Jamie said. She took out the box of kitchen matches she'd smuggled into her room the night before and lit the cone of incense she'd put on a saucer. A sweet, horrible smell began to fill the room. "We can burn it while we prostrate ourselves."

Jamie knelt down, bent over till her face touched the floor, and stretched her arms toward the shrine.

"I didn't realize we had to do that!" said Randy. "I thought we could just sit here!"

"No. We have to do things right." Jamie's voice was muffled because she was talking into the rug.

Reluctantly, Randy prostrated herself, too, and then there was a little silence in the room. "What do we do now?" Randy asked.

"Shhh! I'm about to start praying!"

In a few seconds Jamie cleared her throat and began to speak. "Isis, Isis, come to our aid," she chanted. "Grant us the favors we ask."

"Does Isis know who Marylou and Bill are?" asked Randy.

"*Shhh!* She's a goddess. It's her business to know that kind of thing. Grant us the favors we ask," Jamie repeated.

"Set us on the path toward the wedding," Randy chimed in.

Jamie nodded approvingly from her spot on the floor. "And curse Bill Baird with the curse of Amenhotep," she added. "Make sure he is attacked by wild beasts, especially. Please do not disappoint us, Isis. We have been searching for so — "

The doorknob rattled.

"What stinks in here?" shouted Margaret, shoving Jamie's door open. "Hey, what are you guys *doing*?"

Startled, Jamie and Randy jumped up.

"Haven't you ever heard of knocking?" Jamie snapped. "Get out of here! This is private!"

But Margaret wasn't listening. She was staring at their shrine. "Is that a picture of *Miss Duni*?" she asked. She leaned forward

73

and snatched up the picture before Jamie could stop her. "It is! It is! You guys are praying to Miss Duni! Hey, Betsy! Get in here!" she called.

Betsy's face appeared at the door. "Ugh! What stinks?" she asked. "Is that incense?"

Margaret was choking with laughter. "They're — they're praying to Miss Duni," she gasped out.

"Not to Miss Duni!" Randy blurted indignantly. "To Isis, the goddess of fertility!"

"Thanks a lot, Ran," Jamie muttered.

It was the first time she'd ever seen two people actually fall down laughing.

Chapter Eight

"Randy, can you hear me?" Jamie whispered into the phone receiver three days later.

"Yes, I can," answered her friend. "Why are you whispering?"

"Because I don't want anyone to hear me! Why else? Listen, Ran. You know how Marylou's wedding is tomorrow?"

"Of course I do, Jamie. What else have we been talking about all month?"

"And you know how I said none of our ideas to get me there had worked, and I was going to give up?"

"Yes. I know it was a hard thing to decide, but — "

"Well, I re-decided last night that I was wrong," Jamie cut in. "Nothing *legal* has worked. But I can still get to this wedding illegally."

"What do you mean? How?" asked Randy blankly.

"I mean I'm going to put on my magic sneakers and *sneak* in."

"Invisibly? Jamie, that's terrible!"

"No, it's not," Jamie contradicted. "Marylou's the terrible one. This is all her fault, not mine."

"But Jamie — "

"Ran, don't try to convince me. My mind's made up. Anyone who tries to keep me away from her wedding *deserves* to have me come."

"But Jamie, what about Mrs. Proutie? Isn't she coming this morning?"

"Oh, I took care of that last night," Jamie said.

It hadn't taken much work, either.

"Mom, I think I can live with the idea of not seeing you and Dad for a few days," Jamie had told Mrs. Keenan.

"That's not very flattering," said her mother tartly, "but thank you for sharing your feelings with me."

"Oh, I didn't mean it that way!" said Jamie. "All I meant was that I'd rather stay with Randy than have Mrs. Proutie babysit me. If that would be okay, I mean."

"Actually, it would be a relief," said Mrs.

76

Keenan. "Mrs. Proutie was nice about saying she'd come, but I could tell that this wasn't the most convenient time for her. I'll call her right away. It's fine for you to stay with Randy, and we'll find a friend for Tim to stay with, too."

Quickly Jamie filled Randy in on that conversation. "So now no one will worry," she finished.

"Except me," said Randy gloomily. "I just don't think you're going to be able to get away with — "

"Mom!" wailed Betsy from the hall. "I can't find my blow-dryer anywhere!"

"Just a sec, Ran," said Jamie. "I have to eavesdrop."

"Well, is it absolutely essential for you to take a blow-dryer along?" Mrs. Keenan called back.

"Are you crazy, Mom? Of course it is! How am I supposed to be a bridesmaid with *bent hair*?"

"The blow-dryer is in the closet under the bathroom sink!" Jamie shouted.

"Hey, thanks, Jamie!" Jamie heard Betsy rushing off to dig it out.

"Sorry, Ran," she said. "Things are kind of crazy around here. Now, you really don't have to worry. I'll — wait one more minute."

"Mom!" Margaret was yelling. "I can't

wear these shoes Marylou got for us. The soles are way too slick! I'll fall on my face when I'm walking down the aisle!"

"Want me to sandpaper the bottoms for you?" called Jamie.

Margaret poked her head into the room and stared at Jamie in amazement. "Sure. That would be great," she said. "But how come you're such a little merry sunshine all of a sudden?"

"Oh, I guess I'm just happy that you're getting to take this trip," said Jamie innocently. "It's nice to know my sisters are going to have some fun. That's all."

"Jamie, you *never* think it's nice when we have fun and you don't!" said Margaret. But Jamie had already turned back to the phone.

"I'm really sorry, Ran," she said. "Everyone's trying to pack."

"And you're being helpful so they won't suspect anything?" asked Randy.

"You got it!"

"Oh, Jamie, I just think this is a terrible idea! You're going to get caught — I know it! Won't you please come and stay at my house?" begged Randy. "We'll have a great time, and there won't be a chance for anything bad to happen!"

"Randy, nothing bad is going to happen. I'll just be an invisible guest. What's wrong with that?"

"But Jamie, you know the sneakers don't always work! What if you suddenly reappear in the middle of the cake or something? Oh, please, Jamie, I — "

"Randy, I promise you nothing will go wrong," said Jamie firmly. "Now, I have to go be helpful. I'll call you from the wedding, okay?"

Randy sighed. "I can see nothing will change your mind. Well, good luck — and I hope I'll see you soon."

"Of course you will!" Jamie scoffed. "I'm not going to the moon!"

"I know," said Randy. "This is a lot more dangerous than that."

"Ouch!" yelped Betsy two hours later. "Margaret, will you please keep on your own side of the car?"

"I'm not touching you!" snapped Margaret. "You're the one who's squishing me!"

"Girls!" said Mrs. Keenan. "You're acting like four-year-olds! Do you want me to put a suitcase between you, the way I used to do on trips?" She glanced back at both of them. "Anyway, neither of you is squishing the other. There's plenty of room back there."

Betsy glared and slouched down in her seat. "I guess it's just the car, then," she grumbled. "Why did you have to buy such an uncomfortable one?"

"Hey!" protested Mr. Keenan. "This car is only two months old! I've sat back there. The seat's like a bed!"

"Sure," said Margaret under her breath. "A bed of nails."

I wish both of you would stop complaining, Jamie wanted to say. *I'm* the one who's being squished!

Of course that was because she was sitting between Margaret and Betsy in the back seat. And of course she couldn't say anything, no matter how much she wanted to, because she had the magic sneakers on. She was invisible.

In Jamie's hip pocket was all the spare change she'd been able to dig up around the house. That was for calling Randy. The only luggage Jamie had brought was a toothbrush. That was stashed in her other hip pocket, and it jabbed Jamie in the leg every time the car went over a bump.

"Ow!" she yelped after one especially bad jab.

Margaret stared at Betsy. Betsy stared at Margaret.

"What is your *problem*?" the sisters said in unison.

"Girls," said Mrs. Keenan tiredly. "Let's

talk about something else. I wonder how Jamie and Tim are doing."

"Mom, we've only been away for an hour!" said Betsy. "I'm sure they're fine. But don't you think Jamie's been acting a little weird lately? She didn't seem all that sorry to see us go, considering that about one minute ago it made her cry if Mom or Dad even walked out of the room to answer the phone. What a baby!"

Jamie pressed her lips tightly together. I can't say anything. I can't say anything, she told herself over and over.

But she did give Betsy a good hard pinch on the arm.

"Stop the car!" Betsy shrieked. "There's a mouse in here! It just bit me!"

With a screech Mr. Keenan pulled over to the side of the highway. "Okay, everyone out," he said between clenched teeth. "I'll deal with the mouse."

He jumped out of the car, opened the trunk, and pulled out his tennis racket.

Oh, no, thought Jamie. What if he whacks me with that thing? She pulled herself back against the seat as far as she could go.

Holding the tennis racket high, Mr. Keenan yanked open the door on Betsy's side.

"What are you going to do if you find it?" said Margaret.

81

"What does it look as though I'm going to do?" asked Mr. Keenan. He bent down to peer under the seat. Quickly Jamie pulled her legs out of his way.

"But Dad, that would be cruel! It's not the mouse's fault it got trapped in our car!" Margaret wailed.

Mr. Keenan straightened up. "It's not the mouse's fault it got trapped in your sister's imagination, you mean," he said crossly. "There's no mouse here, Betsy. There never has been a mouse here, and there never will *be* a mouse here. You may take your seats again, ladies. And until we arrive at the motel I want complete silence from both of you."

"Well, here we are!" said Mrs. Keenan in a falsely bright voice as they pulled up in front of the Bide-a-Wee Motel. "It looks lovely, doesn't it?"

No one answered. The motel was dingy and desolate-looking, like one of those movie motels where the owners go crazy and strangle the guests during stormy nights.

"Anyway, I'm sure it's nice on the inside," said Mrs. Keenan after a minute. "Now, Margaret and Betsy, you'll be sharing a room, and Dad and I will be down the hall from you."

"Do they have a pool here?" asked Margaret.

"I think so," said her mother. "An indoor one."

"Well, that's better than nothing," said Betsy, scrambling out of the car. "Let's go swimming!"

Jamie followed her family eagerly to the clerk's desk. She couldn't wait to go swimming invisibly.

"We've got two rooms reserved," Mr. Keenan told the clerk. "One for me and my wife, and one for our two daughters."

The clerk looked confused. "Don't you mean your three daughters?"

"Well, I *have* three daughters, yes, but only two of them came with me today," said Mr. Keenan.

"What about the one behind — "

Jamie turned and bolted out the door. She had just realized that she had reappeared.

Why does the magic always give out at the wrong time? she asked herself as she raced around the corner of the motel. (Luckily the magic sneakers made her go extra-fast even though the invisibility had worn off.) And what am I supposed to do with myself until I disappear again?

Jamie sighed. She had no choice but to hide. Maybe there are some video games in the basement, she thought without much hope.

But somehow she doubted it. If there was anything in the basement of *this* motel, it was the skeletons of murdered guests.

"What a great dinner," said Margaret as she unlocked the door to the girls' room. "Mom and Dad are being really nice about this whole trip."

"They sure are," agreed Betsy. "I'm glad we were invited."

Not me, thought Jamie tiredly from behind Betsy. I wish Marylou had never *met* The Moose.

Jamie had turned invisible again only ten minutes ago. For five hours she'd had to keep out of sight. She was hungry and tired. This would be a perfect time to sneak some real food out of the restaurant — but by now the restaurant had closed for the night.

I'll just have to wait until breakfast, Jamie thought.

She followed her sisters into the room and crawled under Margaret's bed. She wanted to take her sneakers off and she didn't want anyone to see her.

"Margaret, do you have the feeling that — that someone is watching us?" asked Betsy uneasily as the two sisters climbed into bed.

84

"Well, yes," admitted Margaret, "but I'm sure it's just because I've seen too many horror movies. Good night, Betsy."

" 'Night," said Betsy.

And good night to me, thought Jamie drowsily. She was so tired that even the dusty floor felt comfortable. She fell asleep right away.

And she didn't wake up until the next morning, when the maid vacuuming under the bed took one look at her and screamed, "A STOWAWAY!"

Chapter Nine

"Don't scream!" begged Jamie frantically. "I'm not a stowaway! I'm just a regular guest!"

The maid switched off the vacuum cleaner and stared openmouthed at her.

Jamie hoped her laugh sounded more natural than it felt. "I was just looking for my — toothbrush," she said. "It was such hard work that I got tired and fell asleep. I'm sure that's happened to you, hasn't it?"

She scrambled out from under the bed, holding her sneakers. Luckily there was no sign of her sisters. They were probably in the restaurant. "Well, I guess I'll go get some breakfast," she said.

The maid was still staring at her. "You mean lunch." she said. "It's one o'clock, you know."

One o'clock! The wedding was in half an hour!

"How could I have slept so long?" Jamie groaned. "They'll be leaving any minute! I guess I'll just hop into the shower and — "

Then Jamie froze. She could hear her sisters coming down the hall.

"Yup, I'll just hop into the shower," she repeated as calmly as she could. Then she dashed into the bathroom and locked the door.

Jamie glanced into the mirror — and groaned. She looked *much* too much like someone who'd spent the night under a bed. But there was no time to clean up. Margaret and Betsy had just walked into their bedroom. Any second now they'd be trying to get into the bathroom themselves.

Jamie jumped into the shower stall and crouched behind the curtain. Maybe they won't see me behind here, she thought anxiously. And if I can just get my sneakers on —

"I have to get my mascara," she heard Betsy saying. Then the bathroom doorknob rattled.

"Hey!" Betsy said. "The door's locked! Is someone in there?"

Jamie held her breath. Was the maid still in the bedroom? Would she say anything about Jamie? Why would she? Jamie thought in a panic. She doesn't know I'm not supposed to be here!

But there was no answer. The maid must have left the room.

"I can't get this door open!" Betsy said frantically. "And we'll be late to the wedding if we don't get going!"

"Here, let me help!" Jamie heard Margaret say. The door banged and rattled on its hinges. "Maybe we should get Dad to *kick* it in," Margaret suggested.

"Well, go get him, then!" wailed Betsy. "Just hurry, whatever you do!"

Jamie stared nervously at her hands. They had never seemed so visible before. *When* was she going to disappear?

Then she heard her father's voice.

"Could you explain again exactly why it is you *need* this door kicked in?" he asked.

Betsy and Margaret's voices were all jumbled up together.

"My mascara . . . I have to wash my face one more time . . . look *perfect* for the wedding . . . that stupid lock . . . my nail scissors . . . Dad, just *hurry*, will you?"

"Okay, I get the picture," said Mr. Keenan. "Stand back, ladies. Your incredibly strong dad is about to smash this door to smithereens. One . . . two . . . three!"

89

Right on "three," Jamie turned invisible. Without pausing for a second, she vaulted out of the shower and whipped open the door.

Mr. Keenan came sailing through the air and landed with his head in the bathroom wastebasket.

"Dad, are you okay?" Betsy screamed.

Slowly Mr. Keenan sat up. He picked a lipstick-stained Kleenex off the top of his head, rubbed a hand over his eyes, and stared tiredly up at his daughters. Now Jamie saw that he'd already dressed for the wedding. Sorry, Dad, she thought with a wince. You still look *pretty* nice.

"I — I guess the door wasn't locked after all," said Betsy in a small voice.

"I guess you've got two minutes to use this bathroom before we have to leave," was all Mr. Keenan answered. "See you in the car."

"Where have you *been*?" Marylou shrieked at the Keenans as they came panting up the church walkway. Jamie, still invisible, was right next to her sisters.

Marylou was standing in the church doorway in her bathrobe and white high heels. She didn't seem to care how ridiculous she looked. "Everyone else is here! We've been waiting and waiting for you! How do you expect the wedding to start without two of the bridesmaids?"

"Sorry, honey," said Mrs. Keenan. "We got a little behind."

Marylou refused to be mollified. "Do you have your dresses?" she asked Betsy and Margaret.

Margaret showed her the two dress bags she was carrying. "I just hope they're not too rumpled," she said. "The back seat of our car is like a — a trash compactor or something."

Marylou was already halfway down the hall. "Come on! Come on! We're getting dressed in one of the Sunday school rooms," she called back over her shoulder.

Betsy and Margaret raced down the hall after Marylou, and Jamie was right behind them.

"Girls, here are my cousins at last," said Marylou when they reached the Sunday school room. "Betsy — Margaret — here are Robin, Muffin, and Binkie. And you know Pauline, of course."

The room where Marylou and the bridesmaids were getting ready looked like a bombed clothing factory. The three other bridesmaids were busy helping each other into their dresses, and Pauline — who was already dressed — was perched on top of a desk swinging her feet back and forth.

"Don't I look *adorable*? Don't you just wish

91

you could *eat* me?" she asked the second she saw Betsy and Margaret.

Jamie had been hoping, somehow, that Marylou had picked a horrible flower girl dress for Pauline — something brownish-gray with lots of stains and rips and big ugly men's shoes. Unfortunately, Pauline looked exactly like a girl in a fairy tale. She was wearing a long, pink, puff-sleeved dress with a sash tied in a big bow.

Oh, why couldn't it have been *me*? Jamie mourned.

"My mommy says I'm the sweetest thing she's ever seen," Pauline chattered. "Nick's really nervous. He barfed on the way to the church. Right out the car window."

"Pauline!" said Marylou angrily. "Why'd you have to tell me *that*?"

As Pauline hopped down from her desk, Jamie couldn't resist tripping her just a tiny bit. Pauline went sprawling onto Marylou's bouquet.

"*Pauline!*" screamed Marylou. "Be careful! A bouquet is very, very important at a wedding!"

"Sorry," muttered Pauline.

Margaret helped Pauline to her feet and straightened her dress. Then she handed the bouquet to Marylou. "It's fine," she said.

"No thanks to Pauline," snapped Marylou.

She placed the bouquet tenderly next to her while Pauline zipped up her dress. Then she stepped to the center of the room and struck a pose. "How do I look?" she asked.

"Oh, Marylou, you're beautiful," said Betsy. "Moose — I mean Nick — is just going to be amazed."

"Nick was hoping your dress wouldn't have a long train," put in Pauline. "He says wedding dress trains make it look as though the bride is dragging a rug along."

There was a painful silence in the room. The train on Marylou's dress was very, very long.

"Well, he — he won't think that with *this* train," said Margaret. The other bridesmaids quickly chimed in their agreement. "It's much too — uh — too dainty for that," said Robin. "Besides, he'll be bowled over by how pretty the dress is from the front."

"That reminds me! My makeup!" gasped Marylou.

Hey, I can help with this! thought Jamie. And she helped Marylou give herself a big red clown's mouth with her lipstick. Then, the minute Marylou had cleaned off the clown's mouth, Jamie helped her spill a whole bottle of perfume on her shoes.

There, Marylou, she thought. *Now* you're ready.

Choking and gasping, Betsy ran to open a window. "I think the smell will die down once we get a little fresh air in here," she wheezed.

"Oh, the perfume doesn't matter," said Marylou. "It's my favorite brand — Intense Rose. Now everyone will know I'm coming down the aisle even before they see me. It's kind of like my own personal aura. You know, I think it's very, very important to have a — "

"Girls, are you ready?" It was Marylou's mother, Jamie's Aunt Linda. "Everyone's waiting for you!"

With a rustle of taffeta, the bridesmaids and Pauline began to move down the hall.

"Now, everyone remember to smile when you're walking down the aisle!" said Betsy nervously. "Nothing looks worse than a scared bridesmaid!"

"*No!*" said Marylou instantly. "No one should smile except me! I want everyone paying attention to *me*, not to a bunch of dumb bridesmaids! You all just keep your mouths *plain*. It's very, very important for me to be the center of attention.

"Come to think of it," Marylou went on, "I'm going to make a last-minute change in the ceremony. *I* want to be first in line. Pauline and the bridesmaids can come in after me."

All five bridesmaids stared at her in dis-

94

may. "But that's not how we rehearsed it!" said Margaret.

"So what?" Marylou asked in a surly voice. "I'm the bride, aren't I? It's *my* wedding, isn't it? You're just my attendants, aren't you? So why shouldn't I go in ahead of you?"

The processional music began before anyone could answer her. Marylou put on a big, glassy-eyed smile and gave Pauline a little pat on the shoulder. "Now come in right after me, honey," she said. "And remember, you're helping to set the tone for the whole wedding!"

"The *adorable* tone," said Pauline proudly. She adjusted her bouquet and stepped out into the aisle.

Jamie darted out after her.

I'm the one who will set the *invisible* tone for the whole wedding, she thought.

Stepping firmly on Marylou's train, Jamie reached back to untie Pauline's sash.

Chapter Ten

"Pauline! My train! My *train*! I can't move!" hissed Marylou. But Pauline was too busy scattering rose petals to hear her. She marched on, unheeding, her sash hanging limply down at her sides. Only when she'd collided with Marylou did she stop and look around in confusion.

"Get off my train!" said Marylou fiercely, giving Pauline a little push. Pauline wobbled backwards — and dropped her basket of rose petals. They cascaded to the ground in a graceful shower.

The organ music wavered to a stop just in time for everyone to hear Marylou shout, "Pick them *up*, you idiot!"

"It's not my fault I dropped them! You pushed me!" Pauline shouted back.

"Honey, just forget about the tulip bulbs and get up here!" called Nick.

Once again the music blared through the church. Crimson-faced, Marylou began walking down the aisle again. "Rose petals, not tulip bulbs!" she muttered angrily.

Jamie darted ahead of her and ran up to stand next to Nick. "Wow! Great dress!" Jamie heard him mutter moose-ishly when she got up to the altar herself. "Hey, where'd all the bridesmaids go? Aren't they supposed to be in front of the bride?"

Marylou was beaming from ear to ear. She reached the altar, took Nick's thick arm firmly, and stared expectantly at the minister.

Now all the bridesmaids were lined up. The minister glanced doubtfully at Marylou's perfumey feet and then opened his prayer book.

"Dearly beloved," he began, "we are gathered together today — families, friends, and I, Father Steve — to witness the union of Marylou Dawn and Nicholas Brad in holy matrimony . . . "

Well, that's all the ceremony *I* want to hear, thought Jamie. I guess it's time to have some fun.

There was a huge flower arrangement on the altar behind the minister. Very quietly Jamie stepped over to it and picked it up.

97

Then she began waving it gently through the air.

At first no one noticed. Then Jamie saw a little frown stealing across Mr. Keenan's face. He stared at the flowers for a second and rubbed his eyes. Jamie wiggled the vase a little. Her father nudged her mother and gestured toward the flowers. Jamie lifted the vase into the air — and held it there.

Now there were whispers popping up here and there through the congregation. "Is this part of the entertainment?" Jamie heard someone say. Someone else giggled. Jamie lifted the vase another few inches, then dropped it abruptly and caught it just before it hit the floor. This time she heard giggles all through the church.

Father Steve glanced reprovingly out at the congregation. Then a flicker of movement caught his eye, too. It was Jamie, invisibly raising and lowering the vase of flowers.

"Marriage is a sacred undertaking," Father Steve said, his eyes fixed on the vase. Jamie gave it a little spin. Father Steve glanced confusedly at Marylou as if he was wondering whether this was something she'd planned. But Marylou was staring glassily ahead. She hadn't even noticed the vase.

"If any one here present can show just cause why this couple may not lawfully be

98

joined, let him speak now or forever hold his vase. I mean, his *peace*." Father Steve cleared his throat and began again. "Let him speak now or forever hold his *peace*."

Jamie cleared her throat ominously. Nick jumped as though he'd been shot, and Marylou gasped. Everyone in the congregation looked around to see who'd made the noise.

Jamie made a noise like a siren.

"May I ask who is attempting to object?" asked Father Steve.

Jamie roared like a lion.

"Are you trying to object in some kind of code?" asked Father Steve.

"Oh, just get going," said Marylou impatiently. "It's probably one of Nick's friends being stupid."

Father Steve took a deep breath and opened his prayer book again. It was upside down. Hastily he righted it and continued with the service. As he read on, Jamie tiptoed up to Marylou.

"You stink, rug-train," she whispered in Marylou's ear.

Marylou glared at Nick. He stared innocently back at her.

"What's the matter, honey?" he whispered.

"You know perfectly well," she hissed back.

" . . . But a wedding is based on more than

shared credit cards," Father Steve was saying. "It is based on the sharing of that most special feeling — love. And now, in celebration of that love, Marylou will read some thoughts she has composed for the occasion."

"No, I won't," said Marylou crossly.

"Why — why not?" asked Father Steve.

"Ask *Nick*," snapped Marylou.

"Honey, I don't know what you're talking about!" said Nick.

"Oh, I suppose you *weren't* whispering in my ear just now?" said Marylou sneeringly. "Nice way for a groom to act, I must say!"

"Please," whispered Father Steve, "let's calm down a little bit." Then he raised his voice and addressed the congregation again.

"Uh — Marylou will read her thoughts later, perhaps at the reception. We shall proceed directly to the giving of rings."

He nodded at the best man, who plunged his hand into his pocket and brought out a gold band. He handed it to Nick.

Nick took Marylou's hand. "With this ring I thee wed," he said, and began to slip the ring onto her finger.

But Jamie got there first. She grabbed the ring and pushed it back onto *Nick's* finger. It got only as far as the first joint before it stuck.

"What are you *doing*?" Marylou demanded. "Give me that!"

Nick was goggle-eyed with surprise. He tugged at the ring. "I — I can't get it off," he said in a panicky voice. "It's stuck!"

Father Steve waved an anxious hand at the congregation. "If you will all excuse us for a minute — " he said. Then he turned to Pauline. "Go get some soap out of the bathroom," he whispered. "Hurry!"

Pauline stared at him in amazement. "That's not my job!" she exclaimed. "My job is to look adorable and set the tone for the wedding, not run errands. Flower girls don't *get* soap!"

"Well, *you* do," said Father Steve sharply. "Now, shake a leg."

Pauline walked slowly out of the church. In a few minutes she was back with a little pool of liquid soap in her cupped hands.

Nick dipped his forefinger into the pool of soap and rubbed the ring with it. In a second the ring popped off. With a sigh of relief he slipped it onto Marylou's finger.

"Well, what am I supposed to do with the rest of this stuff?" said Pauline.

No one answered. After a second Pauline shook her hands in the air. Liquid soap rained all over the chancel steps. Calmly she wiped her hands on Marylou's train and stepped back into her spot.

Before Marylou could react, her maid of honor had handed her Nick's ring. Marylou grabbed Nick's hand and jammed the ring onto his finger as far as it would go.

"With this ring I thee wed," she said ferociously.

Then she turned to Father Steve. "Cut it short," she ordered.

Father Steve heaved a huge sigh of relief. "By the authority vested in me by the state, I pronounce that Nicholas and Marylou are husband and wife," he said. He turned to Nick. "You may kiss the bride," he said.

Grinning from ear to ear, Nick turned to his new wife. But just as he was about to take her in his arms, Jamie gave him a little shove.

Nick stumbled and fell flat on his face at Marylou's feet.

Marylou hauled him up by the shoulders. "This is all *your* fault!" she shrieked.

"Honey, I didn't do anything!" pleaded Nick.

Father Steve nodded frantically at the organist. "Hit it!" he mouthed.

A glorious burst of music filled the church.

Marylou tightened her lips and took Nick's arm again. Grimly she began to drag him down the chancel steps. It was just pure bad luck that she stepped in the liquid soap. Her feet flew out from under her, and she landed with a *whump* on the floor. Nick landed next to her. And the rest of the wedding party — who'd been following Nick and Marylou — skidded on the soap and piled up on top of the happy couple.

I don't know why people always cry at weddings, Jamie thought. They make *me* laugh.

Chapter Eleven

Jamie pulled a quarter out of her pocket, slipped into the phone booth she had found in the hotel basement, and dialed Randy's number.

Randy answered. "Ran?" Jamie whispered. "It's Jamie."

Quickly Jamie filled Randy in on everything that had happened since she'd left. "What about you? Have you seen Bill?" she finished. "Does he look as if the curse is working? Is he shrivelling up or anything?"

"I hate to say it, but he looks just fine," Randy told her. "I saw him in the park this morning. He was grabbing some cotton candy away from a little girl."

Jamie sighed. "Sounds like Bill, all right. Well, maybe this is a slow-acting curse. I'd better go, Ran. I want to walk through the reception line. They're setting it up as soon as Marylou gets the soap off her dress."

She said goodbye and went back upstairs to the Grand Ballroom, where the reception was being held. Marylou, Nick, their parents, and the wedding party had just lined up, and all the wedding guests were lining up in turn to shake hands with them.

The ballroom looked beautiful. It was filled with white flowers, and white satin ribbons were twined around every surface they *could* twine around. Mrs. Keenan had brought in dozens of potted trees and hung them with tiny white lights. She'd even found water lilies for the ornamental fountain in the middle of the room.

I've got to hand it to Mom, Jamie thought. She really knows what she's doing.

"Oh, I don't know," said Marylou as if she had just read Jamie's mind. Jamie turned quickly to see her cousin shaking the hand of someone in the reception line. Her shrill voice came across the room all too clearly. "I don't think it's quite *elegant* enough, somehow. I tried and tried, but you know how it is with decorators. Even when they're your own aunt, they just don't go the distance."

Jamie scowled. You'll be sorry you said that, Marylou, she thought. I'll *make* you sorry!

She cut into the line right in front of Nick and shook his hand vigorously. "Congratulations, Moose," she said in a low, gruff voice.

"Thanks," said Nick, pumping Jamie's hand equally hard. Then he turned to Marylou with a look of confusion on his broad face. "Did I just shake hands with *you*?" he asked.

"Nick, what are you talking about? Of course you — Ouch! Let go of me!"

Jamie was treating Marylou to the Invisible Keenan Hand-Squeeze.

"What's the matter, honey?" Marylou's mother called from her place in line.

"I've — I've got some kind of cramp in my hand! It feels as though someone's holding onto me. It won't stop!" Marylou tried desperately to free her hand from Jamie's, but Jamie held on tight.

"You're a little overwrought, honey," said Aunt Linda kindly.

"Mom, this isn't stress! I think I'm paralyzed or something. Call a doctor!" wailed Marylou.

Time for your walk, Marylou! Jamie said to herself. Suddenly she pulled Marylou out of the line and began dragging her across the ballroom floor.

"Help me, someone!" wailed Marylou.

There was a sudden silence in the Grand Ballroom. Even the waiters paused, their sil-

106

ver trays of hors d'oeuvres frozen in mid-air.

"I'll save you, honey!" bellowed Nick. He charged at Marylou in a football tackle — just as Jamie let go of her.

For the second time that day, Jamie watched someone in her family go shooting through the air. Only this time it was Moose and Marylou instead of Jamie's father. And this time they landed in the fountain instead of a wastebasket.

"You *idiot*!" Marylou shrieked at Nick. She yanked a sodden, crushed water lily out of her hair and hurled it at him as she scrambled out of the fountain. Water was pouring off her in sheets. "*Now* how do you think my dress will look in the wedding pictures?"

I'm starving, Jamie decided. She glanced around for the nearest silver tray. Those cheese puffs look good, she thought. I think I'll have a couple.

And for the next hour — as the bridesmaids took the dripping Marylou away to try to dry her off with paper towels — Jamie ate. She ate cheese puffs with bacon and tiny potatoes with caviar. She ate miniature muffins stuffed with smoked turkey and miniature steakburgers on miniature English muffins. Stuffed clams, shrimp wrapped in snow peas, crab claws, paté . . . Jamie was in heaven.

Suddenly the drummer in the band hit the

cymbals with a resounding clang. "Time to cut the cake! Everyone gather around!" called Marylou's mother.

Marylou was all smiles again. She grabbed Nick's hand and pulled him over to the cake table. Then she turned and faced the wedding guests.

"You know, a wedding is a special, special time," she said, "just the way it said on our invitations. I didn't get to read my thoughts about love during the ceremony because of — uh — unforeseen circumstances. But now that we're all here together, I think it's very, very important that I share them with you."

"Oh, brother," Jamie heard her father mutter. Mrs. Keenan poked him in the ribs.

"You see, I love Nick," said Marylou. She squeezed his hand and looked tenderly at the wedding photographer. "And, of course, he *really, really* loves me. And isn't that what a wedding should be about? You know — love?"

There was a spattering of polite applause. Jamie's father rolled his eyes. "This is even worse than I expected," he whispered. Mrs. Keenan glared fiercely at him. "Hush!" she whispered back. "It's almost over!"

"And I'm going to be the very best wife the world has ever seen!" said Marylou. "And to start with, I'm going to serve him the very best piece of cake the world has ever seen!

And then you can all have a piece. But please keep the pieces small, okay? I want to use the leftovers for our first dinner party. Isn't that a neat idea?"

Marylou picked up a piece of cake and aimed a dazzling smile at the photographer. "Get ready, sweetheart!" she cooed.

Wait! Jamie thought frantically. Why am I letting this moment go to waste?

She dashed behind Marylou and grabbed her hand. Instead of going into Nick's mouth, the piece of cake sailed off into the air. It landed on Pauline's shoulder and perched there for a second before flumping to the ground.

For a second Marylou's face fell. Then she remembered the photographer. She gave him another blinding smile. "Let me just try again!" she chirped.

This time — thanks to a helpful shove from Jamie — the cake smeared all over Nick's face.

For the first time since Jamie had met him, Nick looked annoyed. "Honey, haven't you ever heard of aiming?" he asked Marylou. "See, here's my mouth." He pointed at it. "There's the cake." He pointed at that, too. "Now, they're supposed to get together, right? So what you do is, you put the cake right in—"

"I *know* what I'm supposed to do, Nick," said Marylou sharply. "I'm just — I'm just having trouble with my hands. It must be more of those muscle spasms I was having in the reception line." She turned to the photographer. "Let's skip these pictures, shall we?" she asked. "I always think those shots of the bride and groom feeding each other are kind of disgusting, anyway. Okay, everybody, come and get it! And remember, small pieces!"

Jamie could have gotten as many pieces of wedding cake as she wanted without having to wait in line. Somehow, though, she found that she didn't want even one. Her stomach felt like a chunk of lead inside her. Why, oh why, had she eaten so much?

I've got to lie down, she thought hazily. Just for a little while . . .

Without really thinking about what she was doing, Jamie pushed open the Grand Ballroom's side door — and found herself standing in the parking lot.

In front of her was the longest limousine she'd ever seen. This must be the one Marylou and Nick will take when they leave! Jamie realized. Wow, it's fancy!

Jamie leaned over and peered inside the car. It had three seats, all of them covered with royal-blue crushed velvet. The middle seat — the one for the bride and groom — was equipped with a television, a tiny refrigerator, and a telephone. Jamie saw that someone had already put a bottle of champagne in an ice bucket next to the phone.

But the last seat in the car looked even more tempting. Jamie's stomach was starting to ache, and her head was throbbing. I could just stretch out for a few minutes, she thought longingly. Just until I don't feel so stuffed . . .

Almost before she'd finished the thought, she was inside the limousine. She climbed into the back seat and lay down with a sigh of relief.

Just for a few minutes, she repeated to herself as her eyes fluttered closed . . .

"Well, folks, we're off!" said a man's cheerful voice. With a roar, the limousine shot away from the curb.

Jamie sat bolt upright. Then she shrank back down again, cold with horror. While she'd been asleep, her invisibility had worn off!

"We'll be there in about an hour," the chauffeur promised the bride and groom. "You two lovebirds just settle back and enjoy the ride."

As quietly as she could, Jamie slid off the back seat onto the floor. Somehow she didn't think Marylou and Nick would be too pleased

if they found her.

"Well, Mrs. Seldon," came Nick's voice. "Are you ready for our honeymoon?"

"I certainly am, Mr. Seldon," answered Marylou with a giggle. "I can't wait to set foot on that cruise ship." Jamie heard her give Nick a long, noisy kiss. "Especially with you as my cruise director," she cooed. "Because as far as I'm concerned, you *are* my cruise director. Forever and ever."

BARF! thought Jamie.

"And you're *my* Angel of Love," he said in a sickeningly sweet voice. "The most beautiful, perfect, fabulous woman in the world."

Get me a stomach pump! thought Jamie.

"Do you really think I'm *perfect*?" asked Marylou coyly.

"So perfect that I'm going to kiss you again," answered The Moose.

Oh, what am I going to do? Jamie wailed silently. I'm a honeymoon hostage! How am I ever going to get home?

Chapter Twelve

The next hour that passed was one of the worst of Jamie's life.

This is what I get for meddling, she said furiously to herself. This is my punishment for not being a good loser about being a flower girl. And I know I *should* be punished. But no matter what I've done, I don't deserve to be trapped with The Moose and Marylou!

"You weren't really mad at me at the reception, were you?" asked Nick.

"No, no," said Marylou. "I was just feeling stressed out. It's such hard work being a bride! You have to look beautiful and shake everyone's hand and dance with a lot of old people — honestly, I don't know *how* I survived it."

To Jamie, it didn't sound like a major responsibility. But Nick said solemnly, "You did great, honey. And from now on I promise you'll never have to worry about anything again."

"Oh, Nick, thank you," Marylou breathed.

Then Jamie heard the kissing starting up again. She cringed and covered her ears. And for the rest of the trip she kept them covered.

The limousine rolled to a stop. Cautiously, Jamie unplugged her ears — and realized that she couldn't see her hands. She had disappeared again.

"Here we are, folks!" said the chauffeur.

Jamie peeked out the window. She could see that they were on a huge New York City pier. In front of them was a big baby blue cruise ship, and on its hull were painted the words "Love Tours Unlimited."

"Oh, Nick, it looks perfect!" sighed Marylou. "I can't wait to get home again so we can tell everyone about our trip. They'll all die of jealousy. Can we go aboard right now?"

"We sure can, honey," said Nick gallantly. "I'll just get our suitcases."

He reached into the front seat and lifted them out. Then — holding the suitcases in one hand — he dashed around to Marylou's door. Jamie was right behind him.

Nick opened Marylou's door with a flourish. And as he did so, Jamie reached forward and knocked the suitcases to the pavement. One of them sprang open — and unless Nick had packed an entire suitcase full of frilly underwear, the suitcase was Marylou's.

Well, Jamie thought, I didn't get to throw any *rice* at the reception . . .

She reached into the suitcase, scooped up a huge pile of underwear, and flung it into the air. The bits of lace and silk fluttered away in the breeze like butterflies.

"Hey, look, Karen! Free bras!" called a woman to her friend.

Well, I think it's time to say goodbye to the newlyweds, thought Jamie.

She began to saunter down the street — and then turned back for one more look. Her last glimpse of her cousin was the look on Marylou's face as Nick accidentally stepped on her other suitcase and crushed it.

Jamie started through the crowded streets, trying to ignore the panicky feeling in her throat. Now, let's see, she thought. I've got to be back at the motel before Mom and Dad and the girls leave. What's the best way to get there without spending more than a quarter?

Luckily Jamie had been to New York several times with her mother, and she knew the name of the bus line they always used to get home. The town where the wedding had been held was on the same bus line. As long as she stayed invisible, she could sneak onto the bus.

Jamie walked until she came to the nearest bus stop. Then she waited until the next bus arrived.

"Excuse me," she called to the bus driver as everyone at the bus stop clambered aboard. "Do you know where I can catch the next bus out to Laughing Egg?"

"Two blocks up, one block east," came the bored answer. Then the driver suddenly seemed to realize he was talking to thin air. "Hey, where are you?" he asked.

Jamie didn't answer, and the driver shook his head. "Now I've seen everything," he muttered. "Including an invisible kid."

Jamie walked over in the direction the driver had pointed her. The bus stop was packed with impatient-looking people. In a few minutes a Laughing Egg bus pulled up, and everyone at the bus stop rushed to get aboard.

"Stop *pushing*," a fat lady laden down with shopping bags snapped at the spindly man in back of her.

"I'm not pushing," he snapped back.

I am, thought Jamie from behind the spindly man. I've *got* to get onto this bus. Mom and Dad will be leaving the motel any minute now!

Jamie hunched up her shoulders and pushed some more. It took fifteen pushes until she'd even managed to get up the steps. She wedged herself behind the bus driver and prayed that she wouldn't be squashed to death.

The bus was so crowded and hot that its windows had steamed up. And it seemed as though everyone aboard was in a bad mood — at least people jumped on Jamie when she suddenly turned visible again.

The driver flashed a look at Jamie in the rear-view mirror. "When did you get on, kid? I didn't see you! Put your money in the box right now!"

"I — I can't," said Jamie miserably. "I mean, I've only got a quarter. I can put that in, but I know it's not enough . . ."

"It sure isn't!" agreed the driver. "I'm letting you out right here, that's what I'm doing!"

"Oh, please don't!" There were tears in Jamie's eyes. She couldn't be turned away now — not when she was so close to getting back! "I don't have any other way to go home! You see, I woke up in my cousin Marylou's limousine . . . the seat was so cozy . . . it's her honeymoon . . . I ate too much . . . And my parents don't even know I went to the wedding!" she finished miserably. "If I can't get back to the motel, they'll leave without me!"

The driver stared at her quizzically. "Sounds pretty complicated," he said after a second. "I tell you what. I'll let you stay on the bus. You send me the fare when you get home."

"Oh, thank you!" said Jamie. "I promise I will!"

"It's certainly a pity the way some people will let hardened criminals twist them around their little fingers," said a woman in a mink coat.

But Jamie didn't care what anyone said about her. She was going to make it home all right after all!

"And you *did* get back to the motel in time?" asked Randy.

It was Sunday morning. Just as she'd promised, Jamie had called Randy to let her know she was home.

"Yes, I made it back in time," she told Randy. "They weren't even back from the reception when I got there. I just waited for them and hitched a ride home. Margaret and Betsy are so used to having me crowd them

119

now that they didn't even complain."

"I can't believe you didn't get caught," Randy said. "I was sure you'd be calling me from jail or something."

Suddenly there was a knock on Jamie's door. "Just a minute, Ran. Come in!" she called.

Mrs. Keenan opened the door. Her face was very serious.

"Jamie, I was just about to do a load of wash," she said. "I found this in the pocket of your jeans. Can you tell me what it's doing there?"

"This" was a crumpled mound of paper napkins. Paper napkins from the dozens and dozens of hors d'oeuvres Jamie had eaten at the wedding. Paper napkins with the words, "Nick and Marylou's wedding. Love is eternal" printed on them.

Oh, no, thought Jamie. I totally forgot about those.

"Randy, I'll call you back," said Jamie hastily.

"So I'm grounded for a week," she told Randy as they walked to the bus stop the next day. "I couldn't really explain those napkins away."

"But you didn't tell your mother the whole thing, did you?" asked Randy.

"No, no. I just said I'd snuck to the wedding on the bus. I didn't think there was any point in going into the part about being invisible."

"But you don't sound as though you even *care* about being grounded! Isn't it horrible being in trouble?"

"Oh, I don't mind too much," Jamie told her friend. "Getting back at Marylou was *completely* worth being grounded. The only thing I regret about it is that now things are going to seem awfully dull around here."

"Hey, *servant*! Get a move on! You've got a pyramid to build today!"

Jamie and Randy both sighed. They didn't have to turn around to know that Pharaoh Baird was behind them. In fact, he was so close that he rode his bicycle right into the back of Jamie's legs and sent her sprawling onto the sidewalk.

"*Bill!*" Jamie shouted, getting slowly back to her feet. "You just made me skin *both* my knees!"

Bill looked mockingly back at her. "A Pharaoh can skin his servant's knees if he wants to," he said. "In fact, I should really make you skin your elbows too, just to even things — *Oooooof!*"

He had just plummeted off his bike into the gutter.

For a second he lay there face down and

motionless. Then he slowly picked himself up.

"Dumb mosquito," he said, rubbing his cheek. "What's a mosquito doing biting me in *October*? It made me lose my balance."

He led his bike away without a backward glance.

Jamie stared openmouthed at Bill as he limped along. "Randy!" she gasped excitedly. "Did you hear that? A *mosquito* bit him!"

Randy looked just as thrilled as Jamie felt. "Maybe the curse is actually working!" Then she gasped. "Jamie, look at that!"

Halfway up the block, two huge, shaggy dogs were loping down the street. When they saw Bill, they suddenly froze. Stiff-legged, they walked slowly over to him and sniffed his ankles cautiously. Then they began snarling and snapping at his legs.

"Help!" hollered Bill. "Mad dogs! *Mad dogs!*" He was dancing frantically up and down to keep out of the dogs' way.

Randy looked horrified. "We have to help him! This is all our fault!" she said.

Then — as suddenly as they'd appeared — the two dogs turned and ran back up the street.

Bill stood there for a second, stunned. Then he climbed back onto his bike and rode wobbling out of sight.

"This curse is fantastic!" said Jamie. "Oh, let's hurry to school. I can't wait to see what happens to him next!"

Maybe life after the wedding wasn't going to be so dull after all.

If you enjoyed WACKY WEDDING, you won't want to miss ROVING REPORTER, the third book in the SEE-THROUGH KID series...

Jamie's magic high-tops are a big help in getting information for the school paper's gossip column. While she's invisible, she can eavesdrop on all the kids — and teachers, too! The column is a big hit, and Jamie's very pleased with herself. But when she spies on Randy and prints an item about her, Randy's furious. Is Jamie's snooping going to turn her best friend into her worst enemy?